Mystery of the Silent Friends

by ROBIN GOTTLIEB

Illustrated by Al Brulé

Cover design by Mort Künstler

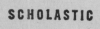

SCHOLASTIC BOOK SERVICES

Published by Scholastic Book Services, a division
of Scholastic Magazines, Inc., New York, N. Y.

For my godchild Mary Jane

Contents

1. An Unwelcome Caller

NINA MARTIN RAN A FINGER along the strings of a dusty old guitar that hung on the wall. In the front of the antique shop, her father was busy with a customer. Nina watched them for a moment. The woman was hovering over a large shiny black urn — the Ali Baba urn — trying to make up her mind about it. First she examined it up close, and then she stepped back to view it from a distance.

Nina's father made no attempt to push the sale. As usual, he stood by patiently, an unlit cigarette dangling from his mouth. He waited silently for the woman to decide about the urn.

"Don't buy it, don't buy it," Nina willed. She

1

crossed two fingers behind her back for luck. The Ali Baba urn was still big enough for her to hide in, even now that she was twelve, and she loved it.

She loved most everything in the shop, as a matter of fact. And now that summer vacation had begun, she could spend as much time as she wanted here. She could browse among the lamps and clocks, jewelry and glassware, old candlesticks and funny signs. She could play as often as she liked with Henri and Henriette, her very favorites in all the shop.

Nina went back now to the corner cabinet where Henri and Henriette were kept. She opened the glass door and smiled at them.

"Hello, you two," she said softly.

Henri and Henriette were mechanical dolls from Switzerland. They were each about two feet high. They were also two hundred years old, but they didn't look it. With their chubby cheeks and curly hair and bright eyes, they looked for all the world like miniature children of seven or eight. Only their costumes spoke of a time long past.

Nina fluffed out the lace at Henri's collar and stroked his green velvet jacket. "How are *you* today?" she asked.

Henri stared back at her with his serious brown eyes. He was sitting at a mahogany desk, a pad of paper before him. His quill pen was in his hand, and he looked all ready to begin his performance.

Nina picked up a small metal crank that lay on the shelf beside Henri. She turned him around carefully and lifted up his velvet jacket. There in his back was a hole for the crank. Above it there was a dial, a little like a television dial. It had five settings on it, one for each of the five different things Henri could write.

After cranking Henri up, Nina turned his dial from "off" to setting number one. Then she pushed the starting lever above the dial and moved Henri back to face her.

"Off you go now," she said.

Dutifully Henri dipped his pen into a tiny inkwell on the desk, shook out the excess drops, and then moved his arm back to the pad before him. His movements were jerky but determined. Bending his head over the paper, he wrote slowly: "Henri Bourdon." Then he stopped, lifted his head from his work, and stared out at Nina again.

"Good boy — you wrote your name." She patted the top of Henri's curly head.

"More likely the name of his creator," said her father. Mr. Martin had come up without Nina's realizing it, and now when she looked around she saw that the woman customer was no longer in the shop.

"I suppose," Nina said. "But I like to think he's writing his own name." That was why she had named him Henri, after all. "Is that lady buying the urn, Daddy?"

Mr. Martin snorted so hard that his unlit cigarette almost fell out of his mouth. "Not a chance! That Mrs. Featherwell has been in here at least once a week for a year, and she's never even bought a collar button."

"Oh, Daddy, you're funny. What would she want with a collar button?"

"Good point, puss." Mr. Martin grinned at his daughter. "And how are the two H's — in good form today?"

"Well, Henri is. I haven't tried Henriette yet." Nina looked at the girl doll. She was seated at a little desk too, like her brother, only instead of a pen she held a pencil in the air over her sheet of paper. She wore a blue satin-and-lace dress, and her blond hair came down in ringlets.

4

"She *looks* chipper," Mr. Martin said. "Let's give her a whirl."

Nina cranked Henriette up, turned her dial to the first setting, and pushed the starting lever. Henriette then went promptly into action. The fine lace at her wrist fluttered as she touched her pencil lightly to the paper and began to sketch. A line here, a shading there — and soon there was a charming little drawing of a Swiss chalet, complete with a pointed, sloping roof and a wooden balcony all around.

"She's up to snuff, all right," said Mr. Martin.

"Let's see the rest of the pictures, Daddy." Nina never tired of watching Henriette produce her delicate line drawings. She turned the dial to the second setting, and the doll went into motion again. This time she drew a Swiss town hall with a tall spire and a big clock.

"And I'll wager that clock's on time to the second," said Mr. Martin and Nina in unison.

"Have I said that before?" her father asked with make-believe surprise.

Nina giggled. "You say it every time."

"Do I? Well, that's just because I admire Swiss craftsmanship. . . . What's next in the art exhibit?"

Nina tore off the sheet of paper picturing the town

hall, reset Henriette, and said, "That crazy monkey. Look."

Sure enough, Henriette now drew a skinny little monkey with both hands clapped over its mouth. The Martins had always been bewildered by it. Henriette's final two drawings were of a lake and some snow-capped mountains. So what was this speak-no-evil monkey doing smack in the middle of all those typically Swiss scenes? There was certainly nothing Swiss about a monkey.

"Beats me." Mr. Martin shook his head as he looked at the strange drawing. "I've never been able to solve the mystery. All I can think of is that the mechanism for drawing the monkey might have been added sometime later — in this country maybe."

Little tingles climbed up the back of Nina's neck. They always did when someone said "mystery" like that. How lovely it would be if this monkey really were part of some exciting mystery — one that she could dig into and finally solve. To think that her Henriette, whom she loved so, might actually be keeping some dark secret!

Nina gazed fondly at both the mechanical figures. They had been her playmates for as long as she

could remember. "Don't ever sell them, Daddy," she said suddenly. "Promise me you won't sell them."

"You never want me to sell anything," her father said, grinning. "If I listened to you, I'd have a fine business, wouldn't I now?"

"Well, sell everything else if you have to. But not Henri and Henriette. Please."

With his handkerchief, Mr. Martin wiped away a

tear that had rolled almost down to Nina's chin. "It's not very likely, puss," he said gently. "They've been in my shop since before you were born, and no one's ever offered to buy them. There's not much demand for automatons these days."

Nina pulled a tissue from the pocket of her blue cotton skirt and blew her nose vigorously. It was true that her father hadn't actually promised not to sell the dolls. But if no one ever offered to buy them, didn't it come out to the same thing?

"The lake drawing is next," she said. They didn't get to see the lake drawing, though, because a man came into the shop at just that moment.

Nina always liked to guess what sort of things a customer might be interested in. She looked hard at the man who had just come in. He was much taller and thinner than her father — younger, too. The way he stood, with his chest puffed out, made him look like a penguin, Nina thought. He wore a very expensive-looking suit and a dapper straw hat, and he carried a slim black umbrella. Nina made a guess that he would head straight for her father's two hand-painted Oriental screens.

He didn't. He headed straight for Nina's father instead.

"Mr. Martin?" he said, flashing a smile.

Mr. Martin moved slowly forward to meet him. "That's right. What can I do for you?"

"You have, I believe, two Swiss automatons." The man's eyes swept over chests and tables, lamps and chairs, till they reached the corner cabinet where Nina was standing. "Ah yes, there they are. I want to buy them."

Nina stared at the man, her mouth gaping. She *must* have heard wrong. In all these years no one had ever shown any interest in either Henri or Henriette, and now suddenly, out of the blue, here was someone who wanted them *both*.

Nina wrenched her eyes from the customer and looked at her father. He seemed as astonished as she was. He took his unlit cigarette out of his mouth, twirled it around in his fingers, and finally stuck it between his lips again.

"Well now," he said slowly, "I don't know . . ."

The customer didn't seem aware of the surprise he was causing. "May I give you a light?" he asked Nina's father. He reached into his pocket and brought out a book of matches.

"No, no — thank you. I don't smoke," said Mr. Martin. "Cured myself of the habit years ago, but

9

I still like the feel of a cigarette in my mouth."

"Oh, I see." The customer put away his matches and said, "Now, sir, about the automatons. How much do you want for them?"

Nina watched her father steadily and held her breath.

"Well, actually," said Mr. Martin, "I'm not entirely sure I want to sell them."

A scowl clouded the customer's face for a moment. But then he smiled again. "Let me tell you why I want them, Mr. Martin," he said, "and I think you'll stop hesitating. First, permit me to introduce myself. My name is George Ballantine the third." He extended a long, thin hand to Nina's father.

"How-do," said Mr. Martin, putting out his hand in return.

"Now you see," Mr. Ballantine went on amiably, "those two mechanical figures were once in my family. They were part of a set of three, actually. I still have the other one — it plays the spinet — and as you can no doubt understand, I'm anxious to get them all together again, where they belong."

Mr. Ballantine smiled again. "Money is no object," he added.

10

Nina stood stiffly beside the cabinet that housed Henri and Henriette. She felt too choked to speak, and her eyes were getting blurry with tears. Her father had hesitated at first, but now he would surely agree to sell the dolls. After all, if they had once been in this Mr. Ballantine's family, and if money was no object . . .

Mr. Martin glanced at Nina and then said, "Of course I can understand why you'd want them, Mr. Ballantine. It's just that, as I said before, I'm not entirely sure I want to sell them. They've been around so long that, believe it or not, I've grown quite attached to the little creatures."

Mr. Ballantine's smile faded away. "I assumed everything in your shop was for sale," he said rather testily.

"Most everything is." Mr. Martin's tone remained calm. "But I'm not quite sure about the automatons."

"And when do you think you might know?"

"Let's say — in a couple of days."

Nina let out her breath in a long sigh of relief. Henri and Henriette were safe for the moment at least. And she would have two days to persuade her father not to sell them to this — this awful Mr. Ballantine. Funny, she had thought he was quite nice-looking when he first came into the shop. But now if he just had fangs, she was sure he could pass for the big bad wolf.

Angrily, Nina looked Mr. Ballantine up and down again. This time she noticed something she hadn't seen before: one of his shoelaces had a knot in it. Why, she wondered, would somebody who was so well dressed patch up broken shoelaces instead of getting new ones? It didn't seem to make sense.

"Very well," Mr. Ballantine said to her father. "I'll be back on Monday." He turned to go, but he didn't see the stag's head jutting out from the wall near him. A long antler poked his hat to one side of his head, and Nina caught a glimpse of red hair.

It was a funny sight, and Nina couldn't help giggling. Mr. Ballantine, though, didn't see the humor of it at all. In fact, he seemed quite upset. He straightened his hat with a lightninglike gesture, grumbled something, and then made for the door.

Now why should he be so anxious to keep his head covered? Nina wondered. Could it be that he didn't like his red hair? There was a boy in her class at school who hated his, even though she thought it was very nice.

12

The door opened and shut quickly, and Mr. Ballantine was gone.

Nina rushed to her father. "Oh, Daddy, please —" she began, but before she got any further another customer came in. It was an elderly woman this time. Nina watched her anxiously, fearing that she too might want Henri and Henriette, but the woman turned out to be interested only in Mr. Martin's cut glassware.

As soon as she was gone, Nina ran to her father again. "You're not going to sell Henri and Henriette, are you, Daddy?"

He put his hands on her shoulders and looked down at her soberly. "Honey, I've got to think it over," he said. "It would mean quite a lot of money. So before I turn it down I've got to figure out how important the loss would be to us."

"I hope it *won't* be important." Nina turned her worried face up to her father.

"I'll do my best, puss," he said. "I promise you that."

A cuckoo bird popped out of a clock on the wall and said "cuckoo" six times.

"Well, suppose we call it a day," Mr. Martin said, giving Nina a hug. "What do you think your mother's got up her sleeve for Saturday-night supper?"

Nina just shrugged. Her thoughts were still on Henri and Henriette.

Her father crumpled his unlit cigarette into an ash tray and took his hat off a bust of Beethoven. "Starting Monday," he said with a grin, "Beethoven gets a well-deserved rest, and those antlers become my hatrack."

This time he *did* get Nina's attention. She giggled as she thought again of Mr. Ballantine's hat and the antler. She must remember to tell her friend Muffin about it. Muffin would love it.

Nina and her father left the shop and walked the few blocks up New York's Third Avenue to their home. It was a balmy evening in late June, and there was a nice breeze in the air.

Nina tried to stop thinking that she might lose Henri and Henriette. She walked along, stepping carefully over the cracks in the sidewalk. If she missed every one, it would be good luck.

Soon they reached the large apartment building where they lived. They rode up to the sixth floor, and even though Mr. Martin had his key, Nina rang their doorbell. She always loved to hear the chimes that played. "Oh, say, can you see" from "The Star-Spangled Banner."

They entered the apartment, singing the national anthem. Mrs. Martin emerged from the kitchen at "whose broad stripes and bright stars," and sang along with them till the end. Then she kissed them both.

Mr. Martin had begun sniffing the air uncertainly. "Could it be, Peg," he asked, "that you've been slaving over my favorite dish?"

"That's for me to know and you to find out," said his wife with a wink at Nina. "Hurry up, you two, before my creation gets burned beyond recognition."

The dining table was in a cozy alcove off the kitchen. On the wall hung several enamel signs that Mr. Martin had picked up on buying trips. "Snacks at All Hours," said the one in French right over Nina's head as she sat down.

Her mother, sitting below "Home Cooking," served the baked ham and sweet potatoes and green salad. Half an hour later, just as she was dishing out the ice cream, the doorbell chimes sounded.

Mrs. Martin laughed. "That girl's timing is fantastic," she said.

"She has special radar-equipped eyes," explained

15

Mr. Martin, "that enable her to see through the floors from her apartment to ours. When she sees ice cream, down she comes."

"Oh, Daddy!" Nina bounced off her chair and ran to open the door. There stood her best friend, Muffin Reed, looking slim and angelic, as she always did. Her straight golden hair hung down to her shoulders and was held back by a blue ribbon that matched her eyes.

"Hi. What's new?" Muffin said.

"Wait'll you hear," answered Nina with a groan.

After two helpings of ice cream, the girls went into Nina's room. They flopped onto the bed, and Nina told Muffin all about the visit from George Ballantine the third.

Muffin was properly crushed by the news. She too had spent many happy hours playing with the two mechanical dolls. "Gleeps, Nina," she said, "how awful! What do you think'll happen?"

"I don't know. Daddy has to think about it. He said —"

Nina was interrupted by a loud and frantic call. "Nina Martin! Come out here at once!"

Nina shot out of her room, Muffin right behind

her. It was not often her mother called her in that top-sergeant tone of voice, but when she did . . .

In the living room, Mrs. Martin was standing on a corner of the fawn-colored Persian rug. She was pointing down in horror at a large and ugly puddle of gleaming black ink.

"Did *you* do that?" she asked Nina.

Nina looked at the spot. "No, Mom," she said. "I haven't touched any ink for days — honest."

"Then who . . . ? Then what . . . ?" Her mother really looked shattered.

"Don't worry, Mrs. Martin," Muffin said calmly. "I think I can get it off." She bent down and picked the whole puddle right up by one edge. It was nothing but a piece of metal painted a glossy black to look like a big blob of ink.

Muffin's cherubic face beamed with pleasure. "Looked pretty real, didn't it?"

"Very real indeed," agreed Mrs. Martin weakly, as she lowered herself into an armchair. "Though, heaven knows, I should be on to your tricks by now, Muffin Reed."

Nina and Muffin began laughing. Nina's father did too, and soon all three were howling with mirth.

17

Even Mrs. Martin, when she recovered from her shock, managed a few chuckles.

"I guess I better —" Muffin began, but stopped in another fit of giggles. "I better get back upstairs," she said breathlessly, when the giggles subsided. "I promised my mother I wouldn't stay long, 'cause I haven't finished practicing." She wiggled her fingers over an imaginary piano keyboard. " 'Bye, Mr. and Mrs. Martin. Thanks for the ice cream!"

Nina went with Muffin to the door. Muffin said in a whisper, "We'll have to try and keep your father from selling you-know-who."

"Do you think we can?" Nina asked hopefully.

"Leave it to me," said Muffin. "I'll think of *something*."

2. The Mystery Begins

"ONE REGULAR COFFEE TO GO OUT, PLEASE," Nina said to the man behind the soda fountain. She perched on a stool to wait.

"For your pa, eh?" the man asked. Nina nodded, and he filled a cardboard container with coffee and put it in a paper bag. "Tell him Ed says 'hello.'"

"I will. Thanks." Nina's coins clinked on the counter. She took the paper bag and left the luncheonette. The sun felt good on her arms and neck as she walked along Third Avenue toward her father's shop. She stopped for a moment to look in the window of a pet shop, where furry brown puppies were bouncing happily in a box.

The next store she passed was a beauty parlor. Nina sniffed the clean, perfumy smell that came from its doorway. Then she reached the shop whose sign said, "C. A. E. Martin, Antiques."

On each side of her father's door there was a display window, and Nina peered in to see if anything new was being shown. The same blue vases were there, and the collection of painted china doorknobs, the Tiffany lamps, and the decoy Mallard duck.

"Oh, dear." Nina saw something that hadn't been in the window before: the wood-framed clock with the crazy pendulum that swung out wildly in circles. She did love that clock. "I wish Daddy wouldn't put it in the window like that," she thought. "Everybody can see it and . . ."

Just then her father's hand reached out and seized the clock, and carried it away into the shop.

Nina sighed. "Too late, I guess." She went inside, and sure enough, a stooped, white-haired gentleman was saying, "It's delightful. I'll take it."

"You sold the clock," Nina said reproachfully, when the customer had left.

"Funny idea, isn't it, selling things when you run a business?" Mr. Martin gave Nina's cheek a gentle pinch. "That my coffee?"

"Yes," Nina said, lifting the container out of the paper bag. "Oh, and Ed says 'hello.' " Nina crumpled up the bag and went through the shop into the back room where there was a large waste-paper bin. In this room her father kept his overflow, as well as things that needed repairing. Here a three-legged chair lay on its side now, on top of an old table that had to be refinished.

Mr. Martin was sitting at his roll-top desk, sipping coffee, when Nina came back. She pulled up a wicker armchair and cast a nervous eye around the shop. "Who bought what before I got here?" she asked.

"Let's see now." Her father beetled his brow. "Oh, yes. A little old woman came in a while ago, and I sold her a couple of mechanical dolls from Switzerland."

"You didn't!" Nina shot up from her chair and rushed to the corner cabinet in the back. Henri and Henriette sat peacefully at their desks, pen and pencil ready.

Her father laughed. He had already told her that he'd pretty much made up his mind *not* to sell the dolls to Mr. Ballantine.

Nina opened the glass door of the cabinet and gazed in at her two silent friends. "You sweet things," she murmured. She just hoped Mr. Ballantine wouldn't make her father change his mind. He was due back for his answer today.

With a little brush that she kept nearby, Nina dusted off Henri's green velvet jacket. She was just about to billow out Henriette's dress a little more when another customer entered the shop. Taking no chances, she quickly closed the cabinet door and stood in front of it, hoping to hide the dolls from view.

The customer was a tall, dapper-looking young man. He had about the same build and looked about the same age as the horrid Mr. Ballantine. As Nina watched him, she stretched herself as tall as she could in front of the cabinet. He didn't seem to notice her, though. He strode right up to the desk where her father was sitting.

"Mr. Martin?" he asked, smiling.

"That's right." Mr. Martin took his platinum cigarette case from his pocket. He put a cigarette in his mouth, did not light it, and said, "What can I do for you, young man?"

The customer pulled out a book of matches. "May I do something for *you* first?"

"No, thanks. I don't smoke." Mr. Martin explained

about his cigarette habit, as he had to Mr. Ballantine two days before.

So the man put away his matches and said, "Well, then. I'll tell you why I came. I'd like to know if you've got a pair of Swiss automatons."

Nina teetered in front of the cabinet. It couldn't be! Two men in three days asking about Henri and Henriette, when before no one had noticed them for years!

Mr. Martin looked astounded too. "Yes, I have," he finally managed to say. He got up from his desk and led the young man over to where Nina was standing. Miserably, Nina moved aside.

"Hello, young lady," the man said, seeing Nina for the first time. He smiled sunnily at her and didn't seem to notice how awful she felt. Then he looked in at Henri and Henriette. "They're charming, Mr. Martin," he said after a moment. "What do you want for them?"

Nina bunched her hands into fists as she waited for her father's reply.

"Well, it's like this," Mr. Martin said. "I'm not really sure I want to sell them."

The man looked very disappointed. Then he brightened a little, as he said, "Perhaps you'll change your mind, though, when I tell you why I want them. You see, Mr. Martin, they belonged to my family once."

"That so?" asked Nina's father in a strangled voice.

Nina just stared, as though she were seeing a ghost.

The customer seemed unaware of the effect his words were causing. "Indeed yes," he charged on. "There were three of them originally. My father sold the two you have, but I've still got the third. She's a honey — plays the spinet, a pianolike thing, you know — and she does it beautifully, I think, even though I'm no music expert. But to make a long story short, I'd like to get all three of the automatons back together again."

The man stopped and smiled apologetically. "Forgive me for not introducing myself. My name is George Ballantine the third."

Nina gave a little gasp. Her father gasped too, and as his jaw dropped, his cigarette fell right out of his mouth and down to the floor.

Two George Ballantine the thirds! Nina looked this Mr. Ballantine up and down, from his gray felt hat to his well-polished black shoes. She didn't *think* he was the same man as the first Ballantine.

Even though both men were tall and slim and about the same age, their faces didn't look exactly alike. And it seemed to her that the first man had been rather nervous, while the man before her now looked quite at ease. This man didn't stand with his chest puffed out like a penguin, either.

"I wonder what his hair is like," Nina thought suddenly.

"Have I said something odd?" Mr. Ballantine asked. "You both look startled."

Mr. Martin pulled himself together enough to say, "No, it's nothing at all, Mr. Ballantine. . . . I hope you'll understand, but I really don't think I want to sell my automatons. My daughter and I have grown quite attached to them."

"A pity." Mr. Ballantine gazed down at the two figures again. Then he looked up at the Martins and said, "How would you like to see *mine?* I'd be glad to have you both come over — say, tomorrow afternoon, if you could manage it. I live only a few blocks from here."

"Oh, could we, Daddy?" Nina asked. Now that Henri and Henriette were out of danger, she was curious to see the doll that had once made a trio with them.

Evidently Mr. Martin was curious too. "Why, I guess we could make it, thanks," he told Mr. Ballantine.

"Splendid. I think you'll enjoy the performance, especially you, Miss Martin." Mr. Ballantine smiled at Nina. "But I warn you, my motive is partly selfish. I'm hoping that once you see my spinet player, you'll realize what a shame it is not to have all three figures together."

"I won't realize it," Nina said to herself, "and I hope Daddy won't either." She began to regret her eagerness to visit Mr. Ballantine.

But the arrangements were being made. Mr. Ballantine gave them his address. "Shall we say around three o'clock?"

Nina watched him carefully as he got ready to leave. Maybe he'd tip his hat, and then she could get a look at his hair. He didn't, though. He just said, "Till tomorrow, then," and started for the door.

There was a large Zulu spear that leaned against the wall near the front of the shop. Mr. Martin often used it as a window pole for the transom above the door. Nina now ran and grabbed this spear. "I think I'll open the window," she said. "It's — oops! Oh, excuse me, Mr. Ballantine!"

The spear point sent Mr. Ballantine's hat spinning to the floor, and Nina saw that his hair was dark brown, not red.

What was more, this Mr. Ballantine didn't seem at all upset at having his head exposed. He picked up his hat, twirled it around for signs of damage, and then said, "That's all right, Miss Martin. No spear hole that I can see."

"The blade is dull, thank heaven," said Mr. Martin, who then turned fiery eyes upon Nina. "You've got to be more careful than that, young lady," he boomed, "if you want to stay in this shop."

"I'm sorry, Daddy," Nina mumbled. When Mr. Ballantine was gone, she added, "It wasn't an accident. I had to see what color his hair was, and I couldn't think of anything else."

Mr. Martin grunted. "Nevertheless — one more trick like that and you get your walking papers."

"All right . . . They don't *look* like the same person, do they?" Nina asked. "But how could there be *two* George Ballantine the thirds, telling us the same thing?"

"You've got me there," her father said. From his platinum case he took a new cigarette to replace the one that had fallen out of his mouth. "But there's probably some simple explanation. Maybe we'll find out when we visit Mr. Ballantine tomorrow."

Tomorrow was a long way off to Nina. Something mysterious seemed to be going on with these two Ballantine people, and she yearned to find out more about it.

That evening she told her friend Muffin about the second Mr. Ballantine.

"Gleeps," said Muffin, around a piece of salt-water taffy. "Does this one have red hair too?"

"No. I had to knock off his hat with a spear to find out. But his hair was dark brown."

Muffin was sitting cross-legged on Nina's bed. She giggled when Nina described what she had done with the Zulu spear.

"Another funny thing," Nina went on. "The first Ballantine was s'posed to come back today — but he didn't. And he seemed so eager on Saturday."

"Um." Muffin helped herself to some taffy from the box that lay between the girls on the bed. "Nina — do you think this was the same man? Maybe he just dyed his hair."

Nina shook her dark curls. "No. I thought of that. But I'm almost sure they're two different people."

She told Muffin the ways in which the men did not seem alike.

"So then there's a Red Ballantine and a Brown Ballantine," Muffin said. "And it's Brown you're going to visit tomorrow?"

Nina nodded as she took a peppermint taffy and began untwisting the wrapper.

"Well, I'll be down again tomorrow night to hear all," Muffin said. She uncrossed her legs, jumped off the bed, and straightened her skirt and blouse. "I better go practice some scales now."

The rest of Monday evening dragged past for Nina, and Tuesday morning hardly seemed to move at all. But at last the afternoon came. Nina waited at the door of the shop, hopping up and down on the sidewalk, while her father hung up a sign that said "Back at about . . ." with a clock face underneath.

"Four ought to do it, puss," Mr. Martin said.

Nina moved the two clock hands till they were pointing at four o'clock, and then her father locked the door and they started off.

They walked briskly west, almost to Fifth Avenue. The trees along the cross streets were looking full and lush, and flowers in window boxes gave color to the elegant old brownstone houses.

"Number 5. That's the one," said Mr. Martin. They stopped before a beautiful four-storey brownstone house, partly covered by climbing ivy. Railings of polished brass flanked the steps that led to the front door. "Quite a place Mr. Ballantine has."

"Does he have the whole house?" Nina asked.

"We'll soon see."

They climbed the steps to the door, which was unlocked and led into a small entranceway before another door. On the wall to the left were four brass nameplates with buttons beside them.

"Nope, he's just got the top floor, I guess," said Mr. Martin. "Will you do the honors?"

Nina pressed the button next to George Ballantine III, fourth floor. A moment later there came a loud and long buzzing noise, which unlocked the next door for the Martins.

Inside, a graceful curving staircase led up. It had red carpeting and a black iron banister with gold lion heads every few feet. Nina poked her finger into some of the lions' open mouths as she bounced along. "What fun," she said. "I wish we had a stairway like this."

"That's because you're young and nimble," said her father, puffing a bit on the final landing.

Nina reached for the doorbell beside a small gold plaque with Mr. Ballantine's name on it. "Do you think he'll have chimes like ours?" She pressed the bell hopefully, but there was just an ordinary ringing sound.

The door opened, and Mr. Ballantine smiled at them. "How nice," he said. "Won't you come in?"

Nina tried to look everywhere at once as she was shown from the foyer into the living room. Dark, polished furniture with gold trim; thick, soft rugs; gilt-framed paintings on the walls. "It all looks more like a museum than a place to live," she thought.

"And here's the queen of the house," said Mr. Ballantine proudly, leading the Martins to a large, low table near a bay window.

"Ooh, she's a doll!" breathed Nina.

"Quite correct in both senses," said Mr. Ballantine, smiling.

The mechanical young lady was about two feet high. She was sitting on a piano stool, her fingers poised over the keyboard of the little spinet before her. She wore a pink dress of brocade and lace, with a billowing skirt, and her long blond hair shimmered in the sunlight that streamed in from the window. Her mouth was curved in a lovely, serene smile.

Nina and her father circled the table several times, admiring the lady musician from every angle.

When Nina's "oohs" subsided, Mr. Ballantine rubbed his hands together and said, "Well, shall we proceed with the concert?" With a flourish he moved a lever in the figure's back. Then, looking like a proud father, he stood back beside the Martins to watch.

The doll came to life at once. She raised her eyes, she bent gracefully toward her instrument, and then her slim fingers began to move over the yellowed keys. Sweet, delicate notes tinkled from the ancient spinet.

Nina was wafted into another world. The doll was playing a minuet. The music grew louder, and the doll's chest rose and fell as her fingers struck the keys. Nina closed her eyes for a moment, floating on the swell of the notes. Then, gradually, the music grew softer. At last, after four quite faint notes, the piece came to an end. The little performer gave a gracious nod to her audience and then leaned back and modestly lowered her eyes.

There was a silence. Then, finally, "She's a honey, all right," Mr. Martin said to his host.

Nina couldn't find any words. Slowly and against her will she found herself returning to the twentieth century. Mr. Ballantine was looking at her with a little smile. He seemed to sense how she felt. "She has that effect on me too," he told her. "Come, I'll show you something else I think you'll like."

He led the way into another room, which he called

"the museum." It was filled with mechanical objects of all kinds — from his grandfather's vast collection, he told them.

Mr. Ballantine played old music boxes for the Martins. He wound up a girl figure who promptly went jump roping all the way along the mantelpiece. He set off a bear that danced on its hind legs while two gypsies beat tambourines around it.

Nina especially loved the acrobat in white who

did dazzling tricks while balanced on a pole. And she liked the clown who juggled red and blue balls and never missed.

The most striking thing about the "museum," though, was its bird cages. They were everywhere. Some stood on the floor on stands, some hung from brackets on the walls, and others sat on table tops. They were of different shapes and sizes, but all were filled with bright-feathered mechanical birds. Mr. Ballantine started some of the birds going, and soon there was a chorus of cheeping and peeping and twittering as a dozen tiny beaks opened and shut.

Nina didn't want to leave, ever. But in a little while her father said, "Well, puss?" as he looked at his watch. So she took a last fond look around and then slowly followed the men out.

"Well, what do you say now, Mr. Martin?" asked Mr. Ballantine at the door. "Will you sell me your automatons?"

Nina felt a stab of pain in her chest. Had she had this wonderful visit only to lose Henri and Henriette? "Why don't *you* sell *us* yours?" she said to Mr. Ballantine. "That way they'd all be together again too."

Both men laughed, and Nina saw sadly that they

weren't taking her idea seriously. Her father shook hands with Mr. Ballantine. "I'm sorry, but I can't tell you 'yes,' " he said.

Mr. Ballantine opened the front door for them. "Well, I'll drop by your shop in a few days, anyway," he said, "on the chance that you'll change your mind."

The Martins thanked him for the wonderful show, and then they hurried down the stairs of the brownstone house.

"Daddy, . . ." Nina began, the minute they were outside again.

"You can wipe that worried look off your puss, puss." Her father grinned at her. "I think we'll hang onto Henri and Henriette. Our finances can stand the loss of the sale. And besides, I'm not happy about these two Ballantine fellows."

Nina smiled happily. "Oh, thank you, Daddy. I'm so glad." She could hardly wait to tell Muffin the good news.

Muffin was eager, too, to hear about Nina's adventures. The Martins were barely finished with their main course at dinner when the "Oh, say, can you see" chimes rang out.

"Hi, everybody." Muffin's blue eyes traveled over the dining table to see if there was anything interesting being served. She was already eating a banana, and she had a second one in her other hand.

"Sit down, dear," Mrs. Martin invited. "What's that spot on your blouse?"

Muffin peered down. "Um. Chocolate ice cream, I guess. We had some for dinner." That didn't stop her from having some fudge ripple with the Martins. She alternated spoonfuls of ice cream with bites of banana. Then she reached into her lap for the second banana. "Would you like it, Mr. Martin?"

Mr. Martin took the banana. "Why thanks, Muffin, that's kind of you." He started to peel it — or, rather, he *tried* to. But the banana refused to peel.

Muffin was doing a good job of keeping a straight face. Once Nina caught on, though, she began to giggle. Then Mr. Martin looked down suspiciously at the banana. "Well, well," he said, bending the rubber fruit back and forth. "That was a good one, Muffin, by golly." He passed the banana around the table, and all four had a good laugh over it.

Then Muffin kicked Nina under the table and bobbed her head in the direction of Nina's bedroom.

"May we be excused now, Mom?" Nina asked.

"How about helping me clear the table first?"

So Nina and Muffin whisked the dishes and glasses and silver off the table. They stacked them in the sink, disposed of the napkins, and put away uneaten slices of bread. Then they were free.

"Tell me all," said Muffin, closing Nina's door on them.

Nina described her visit to Brown Ballantine's house. She told about his collection of mechanical toys and birds, and of course about the Swiss doll that played the minuet so beautifully.

Muffin grinned. "She prob'ly plays a lot better than I do."

"She's been at it longer," said Nina, grinning back. "Two hundred years. But listen to this, Muff. I have good news. Daddy thinks there's something fishy about these two Ballantines, and he says he won't sell Henri and Henriette to either of them."

"Hooray!" Muffin bounced up and down a couple of times on Nina's bed to celebrate. Then she said, "I sure wish we could figure out about these two Ballantine characters, though, don't you?"

"And how." Nina sighed a little. "Brown Ballantine seemed to be George Ballantine the third, all right. His name was downstairs and up by his door, too. But if *he's* the right one, who could Red Ballantine be?"

"Good question." Muffin twisted her rubber banana back and forth as she thought about it. At last she said, "Look, I've got an idea. This Red Ballantine still hasn't come back to your father's shop, has he, Nina?"

Nina shook her head "no."

"Good. Then when he does, why don't you ask to visit *his* house and see *his* musical doll? You ought to be able to find out that way if he's an impostor."

"What's a nimpostor?"

"*Im*postor. Someone who pretends to be something he isn't," Muffin explained.

"Oh," said Nina. Then she looked doubtful. "It's a good idea, but I don't know . . . S'pose we find out he *is* a — impostor. Then Daddy's liable to change his mind and sell Henri and Henriette, after all — to the real Ballantine."

"I'll think of a way to stop him. I promise."

Nina thought about it. Muffin was generally pretty good at persuading grownups to see things her way. But most likely she wouldn't be put to that test. After all, Daddy had said he could afford not to sell the dolls.

Nina was bursting to uncover the mystery of the two men with the same name and story. Finally her curiosity won out, and she agreed to Muffin's plan.

"Okay," she said. "But if worse comes to worst, you'll have to do some pretty fast talking, Muffin, old pal."

"Fear not," said Muffin calmly.

3. Red Ballantine's House

HENRIETTE, the little girl automaton, was drawing her speak-no-evil monkey. The animal was sitting on its haunches, complete except for its hands.

Nina and Muffin were watching the performance. Ah, here came the monkey's hands, clapped over its mouth. Then Henriette looked down to inspect her work. She seemed to approve, for she gave a little nod, raised her pencil from the paper, blew away a speck of pencil dust, and sat back. She stared at Nina and Muffin, as if waiting for *their* approval.

"Yes, it's a good monkey," Nina told her. "Only I wish I knew why you drew it. It doesn't go with the rest of your drawings at all."

"It sure seems queer," agreed Muffin. She was wearing her long golden hair in a pony tail today, and she switched it back and forth as she puzzled over the drawing. "Well," she said, finding no explanation, "let's see the next one."

Nina turned the dial in Henriette's back and pushed the starting lever. Henriette bent over her desk again to begin a new picture.

"Mmm, look at that lake," said Muffin. "I'd like to jump in." The lake, surrounded by pine trees, looked very tempting to her on this warm summer day.

"Better get your ice skates instead," Nina said. "I think that lake is frozen."

Heads close together, the two girls peered down at the drawing to see if they could tell for sure.

"You're right," Muffin said. "That's ice. D'you see the — "

"Muff — look!" Nina grabbed her friend's arm and pointed toward the front of the shop. "That's Red Ballantine!" she said in a trembling whisper.

Muffin gazed at him for a minute. He was talking to Mr. Martin and did not seem to know that the girls were there. "I'm going to listen," Muffin whispered back. And with that she darted off toward the big Ali Baba urn. She climbed into it and disappeared from sight without being noticed by either of the men.

Nina shut off Henriette and closed the cabinet door. Then she too stole up to listen to the conversation between her father and Mr. Ballantine.

"I hope you've decided to sell me the automatons," Mr. Ballantine was saying. He stood, chest puffed out, jiggling up and down a little in front of Mr. Martin. Nina noticed that his shoelace still had the knot.

"Well, no, I'm afraid not," began Nina's father. "I've just about made up my mind . . ."

Nina could wait no longer. "Won't you invite us to your home, Mr. Ballantine," she broke in, "so we can see *your* automaton?"

Mr. Ballantine gave a start. For a second he seemed to quiver all over. Then he put his hand quickly to his head, as if to make sure his hat was still there. After feeling the hat, he seemed to grow a little calmer. But even so, his mouth had begun to make a downward arc. He certainly looked all ready to say "no" to Nina.

44

Mr. Martin, meanwhile, took Nina rather roughly by the shoulders and pushed her in front of him. "This is my daughter," he told Mr. Ballantine. "Please forgive her forwardness. We have no wish to impose on your —"

"But we'd *love* to see a doll that can play the spinet!" piped Muffin. Her head was now sticking out of the urn, and she was such a surprising sight that even Mr. Ballantine laughed.

"Another daughter?" he asked Mr. Martin.

"No, she's a friend. Muffin, you little devil, you've no business . . ."

"Oh, that's all right," said Red Ballantine. He was smiling at both Nina and Muffin now. "The girls seem anxious to see my automaton, and, well, maybe seeing it will help to change your mind, Mr. Martin. Let me think . . ."

Mr. Ballantine gazed off past a set of piled-up wicker chairs to a "The Lord Bless Thee and Keep Thee" sampler on the wall. He seemed to be trying to figure something out. Finally he said, "Suppose I come by for you tomorrow afternoon — say, four o'clock — would that be convenient?"

Mr. Martin hesitated. "Are you sure?" he asked.

"I'm afraid, Mr. Ballantine, these two imps have twisted your arm."

Mr. Ballantine *did* look rather unsure, it was true. Worry lines still creased his forehead. But he said, "No-o-o. It'll be all right. Quite all right. Tomorrow at four." He made his way gingerly past the antlers that had jabbed his hat the last time. His hand on the doorknob, he turned back and repeated, "Tomorrow at four."

The minute he was gone, Mr. Martin pounced on Nina and Muffin. "Now look here, you two," he said, "I don't know what those fertile little minds of yours are hatching, but let's get one thing straight right now." He took the unlit cigarette from his mouth and used it as a pointer for emphasis. "I don't want any of us getting mixed up any more than we have to with these Ballantines. And I wish you had kept your mouths shut a couple of minutes ago."

"But, Daddy, don't you see?" said Nina fervently. "We're sure to find out now which Ballantine is the real one."

Muffin, her head still poking up from the urn, added shrewdly, "Aren't you even a tiny bit curious, Mr. Martin?"

"Well, I suppose I am," he admitted, "or I wouldn't have agreed to go tomorrow. But after that we mind our own business — all of us. Is that clear?"

The girls said "yes" meekly, and Muffin climbed out of the Ali Baba urn. "Let's see the rest of Henriette's pictures," she said to Nina.

"There's just one left. Come on."

They went back to Henriette and watched her draw her last Swiss scene. Two snowy mountain peaks emerged, and below them came sloping hill-sides and finally a cluster of little houses in a valley.

"It's beautiful," murmured Muffin.

"And how! I can see why these Ballantines would want you, all right," said Nina to the blue-eyed doll. "But, Muff" — she remembered something suddenly — "Red Ballantine didn't see any of the drawings. He didn't see Henri *or* Henriette perform at all!"

"He didn't? How come?"

"He didn't ask to. Come to think of it, he hardly even *looked* at them." Nina stroked Henriette's pink cheek fondly. "That seems funny, doesn't it?"

"Sure does. What about Brown Ballantine?"

Nina thought back to Brown's visit to the shop. "No-o," she said at last, "he didn't ask to see them perform, either. But he *did* seem more interested in them. I remember he came up to the cabinet and looked at them for a while."

"It's odd, though," Muffin said. "You'd think if somebody was going to pay a lot of money to buy them, he'd want to see what they could do."

"Yes, you would. Unless . . ." Nina stared solemnly at her friend as a new idea came to her. "Unless he wanted the dolls for *some other reason.*"

"Such as?"

"Such as if maybe they contained some sort of secret."

Nina and Muffin were both hushed by this overwhelming thought. They stared in awe at the two dolls. Then they turned and looked at each other, their eyebrows raised.

"Maybe we'll find out more tomorrow," Muffin said finally.

The cuckoo popped out of the clock on the wall and said "cuckoo" four times. A couple of seconds later, chimes rang out from two other clocks in Mr. Martin's shop.

Nina cast a worried glance at Muffin. "Maybe he's not coming. Maybe he *can't* show us any spinet player, so he just won't show up."

Muffin was passing the crucial minutes in front of a funny kind of mirror that stood against the wall. When she went up close to it she looked squat and fat, and when she stepped back she became a beanpole.

"He'll come," Muffin said. "I feel it in my bones." She left the mirror and went over to Mr. Martin, who was doing accounts at his desk. "Want to smell my flower, Mr. Martin?" she asked, smiling at him innocently.

Mr. Martin looked up from his paper work. He stared long and hard at the rose that Muffin was wearing at her collar. "No, Muffin," he said at last, "I don't think I want to. Why don't you ask my palm tree over there instead? It could use some watering."

Muffin's face fell. "Oh, Mr. Martin," she said sadly, "you knew." She went over to the potted palm and pressed the rubber bulb that was connected to her flower by a long tube inside her dress. A satisfying jet of water spurted out of the rose and onto the shiny fronds of the palm tree.

Nina came up and began twisting one of the palm leaves nervously. "If he ever does come," she hissed at Muffin, "don't ask him to smell your flower."

"Really!" Muffin looked highly insulted.

Mr. Martin glanced over at them. "Nina, stop tormenting that poor plant. People *have* been known to be late, you know."

Nina sighed and let the palm leaf go. She went

to the door of the shop, opened it, and scanned Third Avenue in both directions. Soon she danced back inside. "He's coming! He's coming! I saw him!"

Muffin began jumping up and down too. She was in mid-air when Mr. Ballantine burst in, and she had to grab Nina to keep from bouncing up again once she'd hit the floor.

Mr. Ballantine smiled briefly at the girls. He apologized quickly for being late and then asked if everyone was ready. The foursome was soon on its way. Nina's father walked ahead with Mr. Ballantine, and the two girls followed a few steps behind.

"We're going the same way we did to Brown Ballantine's," Nina whispered to Muffin after a few minutes. They were walking west along the same tree-lined side street.

"Gleeps," said Muffin, "do you s'pose they both live in the same place?"

"Oh no, they couldn't." It was bad enough having two men with the same name telling the same story about a musical automaton. If they lived in the same house, that would just be too much, Nina thought.

They all walked on briskly until they got almost

51

to Fifth Avenue. Then Mr. Ballantine stopped, waved his hand at a building, and said, "Here we are."

It was the very same brownstone house that the other Ballantine lived in!

If Mr. Martin was as surprised as Nina, he did a good job of not showing it. "Are you with us, girls?" he turned to ask them before following Mr. Ballantine up the stone steps.

"It *is* the same house," Nina squeaked, clutching Muffin's arm. Her legs went all rubbery as she climbed up to the front door. Maybe, though, there was some simple explanation after all. Maybe *this* Mr. Ballantine lived on another floor of the building.

Nina looked at the four nameplates as she went by the entrance-way. There was a Horace White, a Mrs. L. Adams, a Franklin Crozier — and only *one* George Ballantine III.

On the party trooped, up the carpeted staircase with its iron railing, until they got to the top floor. Mr. Ballantine took out his key and opened the door to the apartment — the very same apartment that Nina and her father had visited before.

Muffin's face looked like one big question mark. She tugged at Nina's arm for an answer.

Nina moved her head slowly up and down.

"Could they be brothers?" Muffin asked in a whisper.

"What kind of a father would name both his sons George?" Nina whispered back. "It doesn't make any sense."

"Nothing makes any sense," said Muffin glumly. "You're sure they're not the same person?"

"This one's got red hair, remember?" Nina had just time to say. Mr. Ballantine had swooped down on them. "Follow me, girls," he said. "The secrets will keep, I'm sure." He put his hat down on the hall table. Nina stared at him in amazement. His hair was not red at all now. It was dark brown.

Muffin saw it too. She shot Nina a look of disgust that said, "Can't you even tell red from brown?" and then she moved into the living room after Mr. Ballantine.

Nina, chewing thoughtfully on a fingernail, followed with slow steps. This man's hair *had* been red, hadn't it, the time the antler knocked his hat askew? She hadn't just imagined it, had she? If not, what was he doing with *brown* hair now?

"Here she is," Mr. Ballantine was saying. He waved his hand toward the table where the same female automaton was sitting on her stool before the same little spinet.

"Why, she's lovely," said Mr. Martin to his host. "Isn't she, girls?" He looked at Nina with raised eyebrows, and she remembered that she was supposed to act as if she were seeing the doll for the first time.

"Oh yes — beautiful," Nina gulped. She made little gurgles of admiration as she circled the table, looking at the doll from all sides. Mr. Ballantine must not guess that she had seen it before.

Muffin, who really was seeing the doll for the first time, just stood straight in front of it, staring away happily.

"And now for the music," said Mr. Ballantine. Without further ado, he pressed the starting lever. The doll raised her eyes and leaned forward over the keyboard to begin her piece. As her fingers touched the keys, the same gentle melody came tinkling out of the old spinet.

Nina closed her eyes to drift off once more to a bygone age. She imagined herself in a ballroom, dressed in a long, billowy gown, and she was dancing the minuet with a handsome, though shadowy, partner. Back and forth she went, with dainty steps, until suddenly the music stopped.

Nina opened her eyes. She saw that Muffin was also wearing a faraway expression. Muffin's blond head was cocked a little to one side, and she was staring out past the table to the bay window with its deep purple draperies.

"Well," said Mr. Ballantine, "I hope you enjoyed it." He started to move away from the table, as if to indicate to his guests that the visit was over.

Muffin pretended not to see his impatience. "Oh, Mr. Ballantine, it was heavenly!" she said. "Could we hear it once more — please?" When Mr. Ballantine turned back, she looked at him with pleading eyes and gave him her most winning smile.

Mr. Ballantine hesitated. "Well, all right," he said, coming back to the table. "But just once more. Then you must forgive me, because I have an appointment."

The doll played her minuet again. Nina kept her eyes open this time, and she noticed that Muffin was listening intently, especially toward the end. She noticed something else, too. During most of the piece, Mr. Ballantine just stared at himself in a gilt-framed mirror that hung on the wall to one side of the table.

When the music ended, Mr. Ballantine turned away from the mirror and headed once again for the doorway. This time everyone followed right behind.

"Well, Mr. Martin," he said, as he opened the front door to let them out, "don't you see now what a shame it is for the three automatons to be separated? Won't you sell me yours?"

Mr. Martin shook his head. "I'm very sorry, but I'm afraid not."

Nina and Muffin smiled at each other in relief, but Mr. Ballantine did not smile. He looked as though he had just lost everything that was dear to him. He said nothing more about it, though. He merely ushered his guests out to the landing. When Nina glanced back from the staircase, he was still standing in the open doorway, looking forlorn and drooping.

"Daddy," said Nina, the moment they were on the street again, "how could there be two George Ballantine the thirds living in the same place like that?"

Her father stopped and took each girl by the arm. "I don't know," he said gravely. "I thought this visit might clear up the mystery, but it's just made it worse. Now I want us all to forget about it." He shook both Nina and Muffin a little. "Is that understood?"

"Yes, Daddy," said Nina.

"Yes, Mr. Martin," said Muffin.

"The park's right over there," Muffin added. "Can we go watch the seals for a while?"

"Now you're talking," Mr. Martin said, pleased that the girls had their minds on something else so quickly. He strolled over to the seal pond with them, and after a little while left to go back to his shop.

It was mealtime for the seals. An attendant was throwing them pieces of fish, and they bobbed up out of the water to catch the silvery tidbits and gulp them down.

Nina stood with her elbows on the railing that circled the pond. She smiled as the seals popped up, barking and splashing, to grab their dinner.

Muffin, though, wasn't watching the seals at all. Her eyes were following Mr. Martin's dwindling form. When she could no longer see him, she clutched Nina's arm. "Come with me. I've got something to tell you."

"Is it about the Ballantines?" Nina asked.

"It sure is." Muffin led the way to a short flight of steps flanked by big stone eagles with their wings spread wide. There were ledges just in front of the eagles, and they were good sitting places.

The girls perched on one of the ledges. "Hurry up and tell me," Nina said. "I can't wait."

"Not so fast," Muffin replied. "You tell me something first. What's all this business about red hair?"

Nina sighed. "He *did* have red hair, I'm pretty sure. . . . The only thing I can think of is that he was wearing a wig today." Nina clapped her hands suddenly. "I'll bet that's it, Muff, 'cause you know what I noticed? He kept staring at himself in the mirror all through the minuet the second time. Maybe the first time too, only I had my eyes closed. He was prob'ly making sure his wig was on straight."

"Well, maybe," Muffin said. "Or I guess he could've *dyed* his hair if you're so sure it was red before." Muffin dismissed Mr. Ballantine's hair with a toss of her head, and then her blue eyes began to widen. "Now wait'll you hear *this*. The reason I asked to hear the minuet again was because I thought there was something funny about it. And I was right."

"Well, what was it?" Nina asked impatiently.

Muffin leaned closer to Nina. "At the very end of the minuet there were four funny little notes. They just didn't seem to be part of the piece."

"So what?"

"So plenty," answered Muffin. "You remember how I asked to hear the music again? Well, the second time I was just waiting for those four last notes. And do you know what?"

"No. What?"

Muffin paused a minute to heighten the suspense. "The notes were C . . . A . . . G . . . E!"

4. Following Up a Clue

Smack! Nina bumped right into a man who was reading headlines at a newspaper stand.

"Oof," said the man, turning to see what had hit him.

"Gosh, I'm sorry," said Nina.

The man peered down at her. "No harm done," he said. "Only you'd better look where you're going, young lady. Streets and sidewalks are no place for daydreaming."

Nina nodded. She walked on slowly, trying to keep her mind on where she was going. It was hard, because she couldn't stop thinking about what

Muffin had told her yesterday near the seal pond. The Ballantine doll played four odd notes at the end of her minuet, and those notes spelled out the word "cage." It was peculiar, all right. Why should the doll spell out "cage"? Could it be a secret message of some sort? And if so, what did it mean?

Nina almost bumped into a woman this time. She swerved out of the way at the last second — luckily, because the woman was carrying a large bag of groceries. Nina shuddered at the thought of broken eggs on the sidewalk and oranges rolling into the gutter.

At the corner she waited carefully for the light. She put away thoughts of secret messages until she had crossed the street and was on the sidewalk again. Then she went back to wondering about "cage."

The things her own Henri wrote were all in French. So, Nina figured, if this musical doll was really part of a set with Henri and Henriette, then maybe the word "cage" was French. She had looked into her father's French dictionary to see if there was such a word. There was, and it meant the same thing in French as in English. So she was no further along than before.

Was it an animal cage of some sort? Or an elevator cage? Or a prison, which — she had read — used to be called a cage in both French and English? Nina shook her head in puzzlement.

She stopped herself in time to keep from walking into a conveyor belt that was moving crates of cantaloupes from a truck to a supermarket. She went carefully around the truck and then on.

Nina thought about Red Ballantine next. She was quite sure his hair had been red the first time. So he was probably wearing a wig when they went to visit him yesterday. But why?

"Look out, miss!"

Nina jumped out of the way of a man who was sweeping the sidewalk in front of a Chinese restaurant. She looked at the brass fish that made the handles of the restaurant door. "Why, I passed Daddy's shop and didn't even know it!" she exclaimed aloud. She turned around and went back, past a thrift shop and a five-and-ten.

In front of C. A. E. Martin, Antiques, there was a big truck unloading. New goods! Nina forgot about the Ballantines for the moment and burst into the shop to see what was arriving.

Her father, a cigarette in his mouth, was inspect-

ing a rocking chair that had just been uncrated. It
had a wicker seat and gracefully curved wooden
arms. "Ha," said Mr. Martin, seeing Nina, "you're
just in time to test it for comfort."

Nina plunked onto the seat of the chair and
rocked back and forth. "It's great," she said. "Let's
put it in the back room so we'll be able to sit down
in there."

Her father grinned. "So no one will see it, you
mean."

The moving men struggled in with a huge crate, and Mr. Martin directed them to the back room. "*This* we'll keep in there," he said. "It's another one of Martin's follies, I'm afraid, but I couldn't resist it."

"What is it? What is it?" Nina leaped up from rocker and danced along behind the moving men.

Mr. Martin just smiled his "wait-and-see" smile, so Nina hovered nearby while the men banged open the crate. At last a big, old-fashioned sleigh emerged. It had long runners, a splendidly curved front, and a seat upholstered in red plush.

Nina jumped into it at once. "I love your follies, Daddy," she said, resting her cheek against the plush. This was even better than the rocking chair, and if her father called it a "folly" it might be around for a good long time. Nina sat in it happily until her curiosity about the next items got the better of her.

There was a new lamp with a base made from a French horn. Nina thought it was terrific. And she liked the little school desk from the days of the one-room schoolhouse.

"Here's an addition to our art collection," Mr. Martin said.

Nina watched him open a small square box. He

pulled out wads of packing first and then carefully lifted up his prize. On a base of ebony sat a trio of stone monkeys about six inches high.

"Ooh, they're the no-evil monkeys!" Nina cried. "See no evil," she said, touching the monkey with his hands over his eyes. "Hear no evil." She tapped the monkey with his hands over his ears. "And speak no evil." She patted the monkey whose hands were clapped over his mouth.

"Right," said Mr. Martin. "Look at them — biggest no-evils I've ever seen. Usually they're tiny ivory fellows you can hold in the palm of your hand."

Nina was only half listening to her father. She was gazing at speak-no-evil. This was the monkey that Henriette drew in the middle of her four Swiss scenes. They had always thought there was something strange about that monkey.

And now — what was even stranger — the Ballantine doll spelled out "cage" on the keyboard of her spinet.

First "monkey," now "cage."

Slowly Nina went back to the rocking chair and lowered herself into it. She rocked back and forth in a kind of daze. Could it really be that she had discovered the secret? She hardly dared to believe it. Still, put the two things together and you got "monkey cage." Like that, you had a message that made sense!

Suddenly Nina bounded up from the rocker. She mustn't waste another minute — she must tell Muffin at once. She darted a look at the cuckoo clock. Eleven thirty. If she hurried, she might just reach Muffin's house in time to be invited for lunch.

Nina's figuring was right. Mrs. Reed answered the doorbell, a jar of peanut butter in one hand. "I'm just getting some lunch for Muffin," she said. "Would you like to have some too?"

A few minutes later, Nina and Muffin were seated across from each other at the kitchen table, blissfully alone because Mrs. Reed had gone down to the washing machines in the basement.

Nina told Muffin her idea about putting "monkey" and "cage" together.

Muffin was clearly impressed. She spread gobs of peanut butter and jelly onto her favorite English muffins, which had given her her nickname. "But what monkey cage do you think they mean?"

Nina paused in the middle of buttering a slice of bread. "Gee, I don't know. I didn't get that far."

"Didn't you tell me," Muffin said, "that Brown Ballantine had lots of cages in that other room he showed you?"

"His museum," Nina said. "Yes — only there weren't any monkey cages. They were all *bird* cages."

"Oh." Muffin poured out more milk for both of them and got up to fetch the cookie tin. "Have an apple?" she said, waving at the fruit bowl in the center of the table.

Nina started to put out her hand, but then she pulled it back again. She stared at the apple in among the peaches and plums. This wasn't the apple season and, besides, it looked a little too red and shiny. "I'll have a peach. Save your tricks for my folks. They usually fall for them."

Muffin grinned. "I have to keep in practice." She took a peach too, and the juice ran down her chin as she bit into it. "Say!" she cried suddenly. "How about the zoo?"

"What about the zoo?" Nina asked.

"Monkey cages, silly. That's where they usually are. And besides, the Ballantines live right across the street from the zoo, practically. Remember?"

Nina looked thoughtful. "It might mean some old

zoo in Switzerland, 'cause the dolls are two hundred years old, you know. Still, Daddy said maybe the monkey drawing was added much later — maybe after Henriette was brought to this country. So 'cage' might've, been added then too." She gobbled a cookie and gulped down the last of her milk. "Maybe it *is* our zoo. Let's get going!"

They cleared the table quickly and stacked the dishes in the sink. They were just on their way to the front door when it opened and Mrs. Reed stepped in with a hamper of clean clothes.

"Surely you're not planning on going anywhere before you do your practicing?" Muffin's mother asked. Her tone said clearly that all protest would be useless.

Muffin sighed. "Better come back for me in an hour," she told Nina, as she trudged off in the direction of the piano.

"I'll wait here," Nina said. She was afraid if she went downstairs to her own apartment, *her* mother might have some chores for her to do. Then they might never get to the zoo today.

Nina sat down on the living-room couch and picked up a magazine from the coffee table. She leafed idly through it, as Muffin began practicing scales on the piano.

After a few minutes, Nina put down the magazine. She picked up another, but it didn't hold her interest any more than the first had. She couldn't get her mind off monkey cages, that was the trouble.

Suppose the message did mean the monkey cages at the zoo? What *about* the cages? She and Muffin would just have to examine each one carefully, to see if they could find something out of the ordinary.

Maybe there was hidden treasure of some kind. Suppose they discovered jewels, or money, or a priceless piece of art? How wonderful that would be! Nina could see the photographs of her and Muffin all in the newspapers, with the caption: "Twelve-year-old girls find large fortune in monkey cage at Central Park Zoo."

The scales Muffin was practicing stopped now. There was silence for a moment, and then the piano notes came again. This time, instead of scales, Muffin was playing a real piece of music.

Nina closed her eyes to listen. Say, Muff was good — she'd improved an awful lot since Nina had last heard her a few months ago. She was almost as good now as that automaton who played the spinet at the Ballantines'.

Nina's thoughts lingered on the lovely musical doll. Did the Ballantines know, she wondered, about the four notes that spelled out "cage"? Probably they did. Probably they too thought it was part of a message, and no doubt they suspected that Henri or Henriette held the secret to the rest of the message. At any rate, that would certainly explain why they were so anxious to buy the dolls from her father.

Nina wished, though, that she could solve the mystery of the two men with the same name. She brooded about it, but still without getting anywhere, until Muffin whirled around on her piano stool.

"I'm done," Muffin said with a grin. "Let's go."

They walked toward Central Park and the zoo. New York was growing hotter. The sun blazed down on them from a cloudless sky.

Muffin lifted up her long blond hair with both hands. "I'll either cut my hair short like yours," she said, "or I'll make braids around my head. We aren't going away till August."

"We aren't either," said Nina, swishing at a fly.

"I just hope we get this mystery solved before then."

They both quickened their steps. Each was secretly hoping that in just a few minutes they might make an important discovery.

They ran down the stone steps that led to the zoo. Then they turned right and hurried toward the red-brick house where the monkeys were kept.

"Look," said Muffin, the minute they were inside, "a sooty mangabey." That was the name printed on the sign in front of the first cage. Behind the bars a slender gray monkey with a long tail was strolling back and forth on a long metal crossbar.

"He's cute," Nina said. She watched the mangabey for a minute and then moved her eyes carefully over the whole cage. Just metal bars and bare walls and a floor littered with scraps of apple and bread. She saw nothing out of the ordinary. She looked at Muffin, who shook her head, and they moved on.

In the next cage a yellowish baboon was squatting on a big wooden plank. Above it, sitting on a rung at the very top of the cage, was a second baboon. His tail hung straight down, and he clutched the bars of the cage. He stared out at Nina and Muffin with an impassive face.

71

"If he knows anything, it's a cinch he's not telling," Muffin said. And neither she nor Nina found anything the least bit suspicious about his cage.

They moved on to the skinny black spider monkeys. One was doing acrobatics on his crossbar, and another was racing wildly up and down and all around the cage. He was so fascinating to watch that Nina had trouble taking her eyes off him. But she was here to look at cages, not monkeys, so she went on to her examination of the cage.

"I still don't see anything, Muff, do you?" she asked finally.

"Nope," Muffin said, and on they went.

It was the same story all along. At last they reached the end of the monkeys. They went out the door and followed the causeway that led to the next house, where the apes lived.

They saw a chimpanzee, orangutans swinging on automobile tires, and big black gorillas. All were fun to watch, but there was nothing unusual about any of their cages either.

Nina sighed. She hadn't actually expected to see a treasure chest sticking up in plain sight or dollar bills glued to the bars. But she had hoped to see *something* suspicious.

Muffin's mouth was drooping at the corners. "I don't know what we thought we'd find," she said sadly. "Say, how long has your dad had Henriette?"

"Umm." Nina tried to think. "Since before I was born, anyway."

"And did she always draw the monkey?" Muffin asked.

"Sure."

"Well then. The message may not be two hundred years old, but it's been there at least over twelve years. There could have been a lot of changes at the zoo in twelve years," Muffin pointed out.

Nina nodded. "Yes, I s'pose so. If there *was* treasure here once, I s'pose it wouldn't still be here after all this time." Nina cast a mournful look around at the cages of apes. "Maybe the message didn't even mean the zoo, though."

"What else could it mean?"

Nina was silent. Finally she sighed. "Beats me," she said. "You want to go? It's awfully hot and smelly in here."

Heads bowed, the two girls went outside again. They passed by the seal pond, where two big fellows were sunning themselves lazily on top of their house, which jutted out over the water. Yesterday Nina had enjoyed watching the seals. Now, though, neither she nor Muffin felt like it. They just kept on walking.

At the edge of the zoo there was an ice-cream vendor with a white cart. Muffin dug into her pocket for a coin. "Come on," she said, "I'll treat us to Popsicles. Maybe they'll makes us feel better."

"Thanks," Nina said glumly. Eating something always made Muffin feel better. But Nina's mood hardly rose at all as she sucked her grape ice on a stick. She felt hot and sticky and listless.

"Want to go over to the lake?" Muffin asked.

Nina shook her head. "Let's just go home."

They trudged out of the park. Then Nina stopped. "Wait a minute," she said. "I know what let's do. Let's go look at the Ballantine house. It's right down there."

Muffin thought that was a fine idea. "Maybe we'll see one of them going in or out," she said. She and Nina crossed Fifth Avenue. Just a few doors in on the side street, they came to the brownstone house where the mysterious Ballantine pair lived. The girls stood on the sidewalk across the street from the house.

The four-storey house looked quiet and serene from the outside, as if nothing strange were going on there at all. But of course there *must* be something strange going on. Two different George Ballantine the thirds in the same apartment! Nina squinted up at the top floor, wishing she could see through walls.

"Hsst!" said Muffin just then. "Look!"

The front door was opening. The girls scooted behind the side of a car that was parked right near them. Maybe it would be one of the Ballantines and they could follow him!

A black poodle came out of the door first. Alas, it was followed by a young woman in a flowered print dress. Nina and Muffin sighed in disappointment as woman and dog descended the steps and walked off down the street.

"Let's wait some more," Nina said.

They waited and waited, but the door did not open again. Finally Muffin said, "I better get back before my mother has conniptions."

"Me too," said Nina.

They walked the short way home in gloomy silence. On the way into the lobby of their building, though, Nina said suddenly, "I'm going back there tomorrow morning."

"To the Ballantines?"

"Yes. I can't think of anything else to do, and I've got to do *something*." Nina stared at Muffin, her chin set. "You want to come?"

"I'll be down for you at nine thirty," Muffin said loyally. "Maybe tomorow we'll have better luck."

5. Two Spies at Work

NINA AWOKE to the tune of "Oh, What a Beautiful Morning." She reached out and turned off her musical alarm clock. Usually she liked to let the song play through, but today she was in no mood for it. It wasn't going to be a beautiful morning at all if she and Muffin didn't get some new clue when they went to watch the Ballantine house.

Nina rubbed her sleepy eyes, and an eyelash came off on her finger. "Please let us have better luck than we did yesterday," she wished, and blew the eyelash off the back of her hand.

She hurried to wash and get dressed. She buttoned her blue-and-white-checked dress quickly and then whisked a brush over her short curls. When she came into the kitchen, she saw her mother standing at the workshelf in bathrobe and slippers. She saw something else, too. Mrs. Martin was measuring out neat spoonfuls of sugar for the coffeepot.

"Mom!" Nina cried. "That's *sugar* you've got!"

Mrs. Martin turned half-closed eyes to her daughter. "Good morning, dear," she said groggily and went back to measuring. It was a well-known fact that she never really woke up till after her coffee, so she was likely to do anything before it.

"You're using *sugar* instead of *coffee*," Nina told her again, patiently. She emptied the sugar back into its canister and handed her mother the canister marked "Coffee."

Mrs. Martin mumbled something and started over. Nina, keeping an eye on her for further mishaps, poured out orange juice and got out the bread for toasting. By the time Mr. Martin appeared, breakfast was pretty well in hand.

Nina's father, unlike her mother, looked wide awake. He was all dressed and freshly shaved. Nina kissed him, getting a nice whiff of after-shave lotion.

Mr. Martin sat down at the table under the sign "Home Cooking." "Coming with me this morning, puss?" he asked between sips of orange juice.

Nina kept her eyes on the cold cereal she was pouring out. "No, Daddy," she said. "Muff and I thought we'd go to the park." She tried to sound as if this were quite natural, but her father didn't seem fooled.

"The park's getting awfully fascinating lately," he said. "This makes three days in a row if I'm not mistaken. And only a few days ago I couldn't pry you out of my shop with a crowbar."

"I wouldn't complain, Chester," said Mrs. Martin, who was coming to life as she sipped her coffee. "It's good for the girls to be out of doors. If they want to go to the park, why discourage them? It's a healthy trend." She smiled at Nina. "You missed a button, dear."

Nina examined the front of her dress and found the undone button. Then she glanced at her father. She was afraid he was going to go on about the park, and then maybe even bring up the Ballantines and her promise to forget about them. But he busied himself with his toast and said nothing more.

In a few minutes the door chimes rang out the familiar "Oh, say, can you see." Nina popped up from the table and ran joyfully to greet Muffin. Her joy faded, however, when she saw her friend. "Oh, Muff, no!" she cried.

Around Muffin's neck, on a leather strap, hung a large pair of binoculars. "I thought you'd be pleased," she said. "If you only knew how much wangling it took to get them. But I thought maybe we could see something through the Ballantines' window."

Nina shut the door most of the way on Muffin and glanced nervously over her shoulder to make sure neither of her parents was coming. Then she poked her head out the door at Muffin. "My father's suspicious of us already," she whispered. "If he sees *those*, we're dead ducks for sure."

"Nonsense," snapped Muffin, pushing at the door. "I'll say I've taken up bird watching."

Nina stood her ground. "Dead-duck watching, you mean. You hang that thing in the coat closet right away." Muffin reluctantly lifted the field glasses from around her neck and did as Nina ordered.

"Have a seat," Nina said, waving at the living-room couch. "I'll be right back." She went inside to brush her teeth. When she emerged a few minutes later, she heard her mother shouting, "Chester! Look what you've done!"

Nina rushed into the living room just a step behind her father. Her mother was gazing, transfixed, at a lighted cigarette that lay on top of their beautiful antique writing desk.

Mr. Martin stared at it too. "But you know I never light mine," he said. As a matter of fact, an unlit cigarette dangled from his mouth at that very moment. He looked thoroughly puzzled until he saw Muffin on the couch, her head poking up ever so slightly over a magazine. Then he said, "Aha!" He snatched up the lighted cigarette. Sure enough, it was a fake.

"Peg," Mr. Martin said to his wife, "she's had us again."

Even so, Mrs. Martin checked the desk top for burns. Finding none, she shook her head. "I'll never learn."

Muffin and Nina gave way to giggles, until Nina saw that her father was getting ready to leave. Then she remembered that he might bring up the park again. "Come on, Muff," she said, nudging her sharply. "Let's go."

The two girls rushed out, Muffin grabbing her binoculars from the closet. In jig time they were downstairs and hurrying through the lobby. Outside, they half walked, half skipped the few blocks to the Ballantine house.

The day was not only hot, but very sultry too. Nina looked up uneasily at a couple of dark clouds. "We should've brought an umbrella instead of binoculars," she said.

Muffin was annoyed over the way Nina was pooh-poohing her binoculars. "Scaredy cat," she said with a sniff. "What's a little rain?"

The clouds had passed over, though, by the time they reached their destination. They took up their posts in the same spot as they had the day before, and luckily there was again a car parked at a good angle for peeking. While Muffin peered up through her field glasses at the top floor of the brownstone house, Nina kept her eyes riveted on the front door.

Some minutes went by. Then Muffin cried excitedly, "There's someone at the window! I think it's one of the Ballantines!"

"Quick — let me see!" Nina snatched the binoculars away from Muffin and gazed up at the window herself. "That *is* one of them," she said. "He's tying his tie and — say!" Nina peered even harder through the lenses. "He's got red hair!"

Muffin grabbed back the glasses, but by that time Red Ballantine had moved away from the window. "Shucks," she said, "he's gone."

"His hair *is* red," Nina said. "It's red — so he *must* have had a wig on last time."

"I can't see a thing," complained Muffin from behind the binoculars.

"Maybe he's going out," Nina said hopefully. "If he was putting on his tie and looking out the window. . . ."

"Keep your fingers crossed." Muffin had a last look through the binoculars, then dropped them and let them dangle from her neck. "Nothing more to see. But they *did* come in handy, didn't they?"

"Yes, they did at that." Nina grinned for a moment, but soon was serious again. "If Red comes out, I sure hope he won't be wearing a hat. I'd like you to see his hair."

The girls waited, chattering and hopping around impatiently. The street was fairly quiet. A couple of people passed by on Saturday-morning errands, one with a large bag of laundry slung over his shoulder. The traffic was light, too. A few cars cruised by, their drivers looking for parking places. Whenever there was anyone in sight, Nina and Muffin tried to act as if they were taking a walk and had just stopped for a minute. No one spoke to them, though.

Suddenly Nina gave Muffin a quick poke with her elbow. The front door was starting to open! "Here comes someone," Nina whispered, ducking as far out of sight as possible.

Muffin held up two crossed fingers and flattened herself against the car. Just a wisp of blond hair and one wide blue eye showed around it.

The door opened further, and a man appeared. He was tall and thin and wore a light gray suit. He was also wearing a hat. He stood in a way that made his chest puff out like a penguin's.

The girls had time to examine him because he paused on the top step for a minute, gazing up at the sky. Then he came walking down the steps to the sidewalk.

"It's Red, all right," Nina said in a low voice. "Only, darn it, he's got a hat on again."

They watched him turn and go down the block.

When he was quite a ways ahead, Nina said, "Come on. We've got to follow him!" She and Muffin left the protection of the automobile and inched along behind Red Ballantine. They watched him closely, fearing that at any moment he might turn around and see them.

At the corner he met a woman with a dog and stopped to speak to her. Nina and Muffin darted behind a tree.

"It's the woman we saw yesterday," Nina said.

"That's right," Muffin agreed. "*She* came out of his building when we were hoping for *him*."

Red Ballantine and the woman finished talking and continued on in their opposite directions. As they parted, Mr. Ballantine tipped his hat to her.

"Gleeps, Nina!" gasped Muffin. "You're absolutely right."

Mr. Ballantine had remained hatless long enough for both girls to see that his hair was a fiery red.

"There *is* something funny going on," Muffin said, as she and Nina trailed along after Red Ballantine again.

He kept going until he came to a sort of tearoom. There he stopped, opened the door, and went inside. The girls crept on till they were near the tearoom, too. Then, almost at the same time, they both caught their breath.

The tearoom was called The Monkey Cage!

When Nina and Muffin got over the shock of the name of the tearoom, they grabbed each other by the hands and did a little dance on the sidewalk. Muffin's binoculars jounced up and down against her chest.

Here was another kind of monkey cage, not even two blocks away from the Ballantine house. *This* could be the monkey cage they were looking for!

"Funny we didn't notice it yesterday," Muffin said. "We must've gone right by."

"We were too busy thinking about zoos, I guess," said Nina. Through the window she could see Red Ballantine talking to a waitress. He was sitting with his back to them. The waitress went away and then returned with what looked like a Danish pastry and a cup of coffee.

Nina and Muffin drew away from the window. While Mr. Ballantine had his breakfast, they worked out a plan of action.

"Let's wait for him," Nina said. "Then we can follow him and see where he goes next."

"Yes, let's," Muffin agreed. "And when we're through with *him*, we get busy on the tearoom." She gazed up and down the street. "Look, there's a stationery store. Let's go and wait there. We'll be able to see the tearoom okay."

They crossed the street to the stationery store and went in. Muffin made straight for the candy counter, but Nina hovered near the door, her eyes fixed on the tearoom. Mr. Ballantine might come out at any moment, and they mustn't lose him.

A salesclerk headed toward Nina, so she pretended to be looking over the magazines. She picked one up and turned the pages. She glanced up at the tearoom again. Red Ballantine was coming to the door!

Nina dropped the magazine and rushed over to Muffin. "He's left!" she said excitedly. "Come on!"

Muffin was hesitating between gumdrops and a chocolate bar. She looked at them both again, snatched the chocolate bar, and plunked down her coin. Then she hurried after Nina, who had already shot out of the store.

From their side of the street, they kept a careful watch on Mr. Ballantine.

"He's going back the way he came," Muffin said,

as she and Nina moved along too. "Maybe he's just going home."

"I kind of hope he is," Nina admitted. "I'm dying to get to the tearoom, aren't you?"

"M-m-mm." Muffin had just taken a huge bite of her chocolate bar, which made talking impossible for the moment. She held out the rest of the bar to Nina.

It began to look more and more as though Mr. Ballantine *was* on his way home. He turned the corner at his block and started down the street on which he lived. Yes, there he was, stopping at the ivy-draped brownstone house. From the end of the street, Nina and Muffin watched him go up the steps and disappear through the door.

"Okay," said Nina happily. "Mission number two: the tearoom."

They turned and ran back to the little place called The Monkey Cage. Stopping outside the shop, they waited until their breath came normally again. Then they pushed open the door and went in, trying to look properly sedate.

A hostess in black showed them to a small table for two. Then a waitress came up to them. "Central Park bird watchers," she said, seeing Muffin's binoculars on the table. "Spot anything interesting today?"

"Yes. A red-headed puff-chest," said Muffin with a perfectly straight face.

Nina, though, had to dig a fingernail into her palm to keep from laughing at Muffin's description of Red Ballantine.

"Well, that sounds exciting all right," said the waitress. "And now, girls, what'll it be?"

Nina and Muffin stared blankly at each other. What did one order in a tearoom at eleven in the morning?

The waitress came to their rescue. "Something cool and refreshing? How about orangeade?"

The girls nodded gratefully, and the waitress went off.

"Red-headed puff-chest," said Nina. "Honestly." She collapsed in giggles.

Muffin, meanwhile, was swiveling her neck to view the room. "Hey," she said, "you see anything here that looks like a monkey cage?"

Nina inspected the tearoom too. The windows were trimmed with pink café curtains, and the walls were decorated with colored posters of far-away places. Nothing suggested monkeys or their cages.

The orangeades arrived. They were in the tallest glasses Nina had ever seen, and with them came red-and-white-striped straws. Nina was just in time to keep Muffin from shooting her straw wrapper at the back of a man's neck nearby. With a growl Muffin blew the paper into her own hand instead and then crumpled it up.

"You're terrible," Nina said, trying not to giggle. "We've got to behave ourselves in here if we want to find out anything."

Nina's way of finding out began with a second, more thorough study of the tearoom. Her prying eyes picked out nothing unusual, but then they couldn't see inside the big tea and coffee canisters that stood on a shelf above the cash register. Suppose there was a handful of gleaming emeralds or rubies hiding down near the bottom?

Muffin conducted her research in a different way. When the waitress brought their check, Muffin asked her, "Why do they call this place the Monkey Cage?"

The waitress shrugged. "Oh, I suppose because we're near the zoo."

"It's a real nice place." Muffin smiled angelically. "Has it been here long?"

"Quite a while. A little over five years now."

To the waitress, five years might seem "quite a while," but for Muffin it wasn't at all long enough. She turned a dejected face to Nina when the waitress left.

"You told me your dad's had Henriette since before you were born," Muffin said. "And that she's always drawn the monkey."

Nina looked bleak now too. "Yes, that's right. So the message can't mean this place if it's only been here five years."

They stared miserably at each other over their empty glasses. Nina played with her straw, bending it back and forth. "Muff," she said after a little while, "I just thought of something. What if we haven't got the whole message?"

"What d'you mean?"

"Well, we've got 'cage' from the doll that plays the spinet. And we've got 'monkey' from Henriette." Nina leaned forward, her eyes gleaming. "But maybe Henri has something to tell us too."

"Gleeps," said Muffin, "that's right. We haven't bothered with Henri at all."

"We can fix that." Nina looked at the clock on the tearoom wall. It was getting on toward noon. "Right after lunch," she said, "we'll go to Daddy's shop and get busy on Henri."

"It's a date. Only," Muffin added, "maybe I better have lunch at *your* house today. If my mother gets her hands on me, I'll be stuck for an hour of practicing again."

"Okay. But let's get started." Nina picked up the check, Muffin picked up her binoculars, and they were on their way.

6. A Burglar

IN FRONT OF THE ANTIQUE SHOP, Nina and Muffin paused to look at the display windows. They saw the same collection of china doorknobs, the same blue vases and Tiffany lamps, and the same decoy Mallard duck. The windows were certainly overdue for a changing. Nina couldn't remember her father ever keeping one display for so long. Not that she minded. When he changed it, he was liable to put out things that she cared more about.

"Come *on*," said Muffin, tugging at her. They went into the shop.

"Well — do my eyes deceive me?" said Mr. Martin from his desk. "Or are the prides of Central Park really paying me a visit?"

"Oh, the park was swell, Mr. Martin," Muffin said, "but we like it here too." She smiled her most innocent smile.

Mr. Martin greeted it with a suspicious "hmm." As he turned back to the papers on his desk, Nina caught hold of Muffin's arm. "We better not start on Henri right away," she whispered. "I'm afraid Daddy already thinks we're up to something."

So they played with the Indian jewelry for a while. They tried on silver bracelets, turquoise earrings, and pins in the shape of thunderbirds. When Mr. Martin was busy with a customer, the girls finally slipped over to the cabinet where Henri and Henriette were kept.

The little dolls sat at their desks, waiting to perform. It was usually Henriette who got picked first, because Nina and Muffin loved her drawings so. But today they had eyes only for Henri. He looked very elegant in his green velvet jacket, silk trousers, and black shoes with gold buckles. His dark eyes looked straight at the girls, and Nina half expected him to open his mouth and speak.

Henri remained silent though, his quill pen poised

over his writing pad. He would do his talking on paper. And maybe, Nina thought, one of the things he wrote would have a special meaning for her now. She set the dial in his back at position number one, and then she pressed the starting lever. "Please don't let us down," she whispered to him.

Henri dipped his pen into the inkwell on his desk. He shook off the excess drops of ink with two little taps, then bent over his pad and began to work. "Henri Bourdon," he wrote. After that, he stopped, lifted his head, and stared out again at the girls.

Nina tore off the sheet of paper and studied the name. She frowned at Muffin. "I don't see how 'Henri Bourdon' goes with 'monkey cage,' do you?"

Muffin shook her blond pony tail. "Let's try the next one."

In position number two, Henri went through his pen-dipping-and-tapping ritual again. Then slowly, carefully, he wrote in French, "Welcome to Beauvallon."

Nina knew what everything he wrote meant, because her father had long ago explained the French to her. Muffin knew too, because Nina had explained it all to *her*.

"Beauvallon," Muffin said, squinting down at the

96

pad. "You said that was the town he came from."

"That's right." Nina tore off the page. "But I don't see what it has to do with our message."

"Me neither," said Muffin, and they moved on to setting number three.

This time, in his fine, flowery penmanship, Henri wrote in French, "In the heart of the Jura."

The Jura were the mountains near Henri's home town. Nina and Muffin shook their heads at each other sadly. They were even sadder a few minutes later, because neither "Long live Switzerland" nor "Glory to God" seemed to connect up in any way with "monkey cage."

Nina held the five sheets of paper with Henri's performances. "I'm going to take these home and study them some more, Muff," she said. "Maybe there's something we're just not seeing."

"Okay, I will too." Muffin tiptoed over to Mr. Martin's desk and took one of his business cards. She glanced at him out of the corner of her eye. Good — he was busy showing candlesticks to a customer. Muffin hurried back to Nina and quickly copied down all of Henri's writings on the back of the card. "There. Now I better get out of here, or my mother'll have my head. See you tonight."

"Sure." Nina watched Muffin go out of the shop. She folded Henri's sheets of paper in half and tucked them into the pocket of her dress.

"If only you could talk," she said to Henri. She stared at him, biting her lip and wondering how she could find out his secret.

"An automaton for your thoughts, puss."

Nina jumped. "Oh, Daddy, you scared me." She gazed up at her father reproachfully. He was standing over her, an unlit cigarette in his mouth, and he had a funny look in his eye. The customer seemed to be gone.

"Fourth of July's coming up," Mr. Martin said. "Want to help me figure out a patriotic window display?"

"Course I do." Nina closed the glass-fronted door on Henri and Henriette, and tried to close the door of her mind on them as well. So her father was going to change his windows finally. Well, she was glad she was there to help. Maybe she could keep him from putting out any of her favorite things.

Mr. Martin ambled over to a corner of the shop where an old American flag hung on the wall. It had the right number of red and white stripes, but only thirty-four stars. "There's this for a start, of course," he said.

"And those guns," said Nina, pointing to a pair of Revolutionary muskets. She didn't care at all if someone bought *them.*

"Good girl." Her father dug the muskets out of their corner and leaned them against a table near the flag. "And I had a Revolutionary hat around here somewhere, too." He combed through several tables of odds and ends and finally came up with a battered old three-cornered hat.

"We ought to have a head to put it on," Nina said.

"Right you are." Mr. Martin twirled the hat as he looked around for a head that would fill the bill. "Beethoven — nope . . . ah, here's honest Abe Lincoln. I guess he'll do. Of course he came eighty-some years later, but that can't be helped. George Washington isn't around here."

Nina wished she had kept still, because she loved the bust of Lincoln. Just as her father was about to take it down from its shelf, though, the telephone rang. He left the bust and went to answer the call.

"Oh, hello, Mrs. Millenfern," Nina heard him say. "Yes, I see. . . . It certainly *does* interest me." Mr.

Martin looked at the cuckoo clock. "Well, I'll tell you, it's almost four o'clock now. Give me a few minutes to close up, and I can be over in, say, half an hour."

"Over where, Daddy?" Nina asked, after he had hung up.

"Mrs. Millenfern's. A wealthy client. She's moving, and she wants to sell a lot of her furniture. Should be some good pieces." Mr. Martin looked as excited as a boy with a brand-new bike. He rolled the top down over his desk and bustled around the shop, tidying up. The window display was now far from his mind.

"I may be some time, puss," he said, "so I think I'll close up for the day. You go on home."

Nina walked home slowly because the day was so hot and muggy. When she arrived, her mother sent her out again for a quart of ice cream. The cold container felt good in Nina's hands. She held it up to her forehead as she returned from the drugstore.

"Thanks, dear." Mrs. Martin popped the ice cream into the freezer and went back to cutting vegetables for salad.

Nina went to her bedroom and shut the door. She

100

took Henri's writings from her pocket, unfolded them, and stretched out on her bed to look them over again. She laid out all five sheets around her. Propped up on her elbows, she studied one after the other. Maybe now she'd notice something that she and Muffin had missed in the shop.

A long while later, Nina raised her eyes from Henri's work. She stared at the rosebuds on her wallpaper. She felt tired and defeated. None of Henri's writings seemed to fit in with "monkey cage" at all.

Finally she mustered the energy to get up off her bed. She gathered the papers together and hid them in her dresser drawer under a pile of folded pajamas. She stood there hands still on the drawer knobs, looking into the mirror. What to do next? Her frowning reflection stared back at her in silence. Nina made a face at it and turned away.

The only thing she could think of was another excursion to the Ballantine house. Sooner or later one of the Ballantines might lead her onto the trail of something. But who was to say it would be sooner rather than later?

At dinner Nina still felt very low. She toyed with

the tomatoes and radishes in her salad while her father went over the items he'd bought at Mrs. Millenfern's.

". . . and two matching Hepplewhite chairs, Peg," he said proudly, "and a very interesting Chippendale table with . . ."

Nina hardly listened. Chairs and tables, no matter how antique, weren't going to help her solve the mystery about the Ballantines and the mechanical dolls. She welcomed the door chimes that announced Muffin. Maybe her friend had thought of something in the last few hours.

Muffin's usually cheery face looked glum, though. She shook her blond head. "I racked my brains, Nina, honest, but . . ." She finished the sentence with a helpless shrug.

"Ditto." Nina opened the door wider. "Well, come on in and have some dessert, anyway."

When supper was over, the two girls flapped around restlessly in the living room. Finally Mrs. Martin looked up from the novel she was reading. "Nina," she said, "why don't you start that jigsaw puzzle Uncle Gene gave you? You can set it out on the big table, if you like."

"Okay," Nina said without much enthusiasm. She brought in the puzzle, and Muffin pulled chairs up to the large table near the window.

"What's it about?" Muffin asked.

Nina held up the box. "Flower Market in Paris," she read.

"Oh, great. Anybody been to Paris lately?"

"Well," Nina said, dumping the pieces onto the table, "we've got the picture on the box. And I guess we can always get the edges done, anyway."

They worked away at finding all the edge pieces. But after the borders were in, the puzzle got harder. They both lost interest in it after a while.

"Maybe we could make some fudge." Muffin looked hopefully at Mrs. Martin.

"Not on your life," Mrs. Martin said quickly. She had just cleaned up her kitchen, and she knew only too well what it would look like after Nina and Muffin got through in it.

Muffin, however, continued to stare at Nina's mother. She didn't say anything more — she gazed at her with a sort of thoughtful expression. Finally Mrs. Martin broke down under the stare. "Is something wrong?" she asked.

"Oh no, nothing," Muffin said. "It's just that — well, I thought maybe you'd gotten a little fatter lately, that's all."

Mrs. Martin cringed at the word "fatter." "Chester," she asked in a nervous voice, "do I look, uh, heavier to you?"

Mr. Martin looked up from his desk, where he was fiddling with the wiring of a small Tole lamp. Pliers in hand, he peered at his wife. "Um, maybe a little," he said, "now that you mention it."

With this encouragement Muffin jumped up from her chair. "I have a tape measure," she said eagerly. She drew it out of her pocket.

Mrs. Martin couldn't resist checking her waistline. She took Muffin's tape measure and wound it around her middle. "Forty-two inches!" she shrieked. For a moment she looked as though she might faint. Then common sense began to take over. She looked at Muffin with narrowed eyes and said, "I have a sneaking suspicion that tape measure is rigged."

Muffin couldn't keep a straight face any longer. "I fooled you! I fooled you!" she chanted, bouncing up and down in glee. She showed the Martins how extra inches had been squeezed onto the tape measure by shortening the length of each inch. Then they all began measuring themselves. Mr. Martin made the girth of a professional wrestler, and even Nina's skinny middle came to a fair amount.

It was Muffin's most successful trick by far, and she decided to make her exit on this note of glory.

Nina stepped outside the door with her for a moment. "You want to go back to the Ballantines' Monday morning?" she whispered. "I can't go tomorrow 'cause we're visiting my aunt and uncle for the day."

Muffin nodded. "I'll come down for you Monday then."

This time, however, their plan for watching the Ballantine house was foiled. On Monday morning, when Nina and Muffin said they were going to Central Park, Mr. Martin put his foot down. "If you go anywhere, Nina," he said firmly, "you'll come to the shop with me."

"I thought you were giving yourself a holiday today, Chester," his wife said.

"Changed my mind. I want to get the windows ready for the Fourth. I could use some help," he added, looking at Nina.

So Nina and Muffin trailed along behind Mr. Martin to the antique shop. "Maybe we can sneak off later," Muffin whispered.

"Um," said Nina, who didn't think her father's mood was very promising.

Inside the shop, they got busy right away on the display windows. "If you girls take out what's there now," Mr. Martin said, "I'll get the new stuff ready. I don't have to remind you to handle everything very carefully."

Nina and Muffin crawled along the felt that lined the floor of the display area. With great care they picked up vases and lamps, doorknobs and bric-a-brac, and removed them to a nearby table. All was going well until Muffin lost her balance climbing down with the decoy Mallard duck. She just caught herself from falling, but the duck slipped out of her hands and dropped to the floor.

"Oh, gleeps, Mr. Martin!" she wailed. "Look what I've done. I'm awfully sorry!"

Mr. Martin stopped in the middle of taking his American flag off the wall and went over to Muffin. They both looked down at the duck. Its bill had broken off and was now lying a couple of feet away.

Mr. Martin picked up duck and bill and fitted the

106

two together. "It's not serious, Muffin," he said. "It's a clean cut. I can fix it easily."

Muffin grinned her relief. Mr. Martin handed her the two pieces and said, "Put them in the back room, will you? You'll see a table there with some other things to be repaired."

"Sure thing." Muffin trotted through the shop into the back room. When she came out again, she was walking slowly and her face was white. "M-Mr. Martin," she said. "There's a windowpane broken in there — right near the back door. I tried the door, and it wasn't locked!"

Mr. Martin stared at her. "If this is another of your practical jokes, Muffin Reed . . ." he said, but followed her into the back room nevertheless. Nina jumped down from the display window and ran in too.

They all three stood looking at the broken glass on the floor and at the jagged hole in the windowpane just to the left of the back door. Then Mr. Martin tried the door. It was unlocked.

"My apologies to you, Muffin," he said.

"Did you maybe forget to lock it, Daddy?" Nina asked.

"I don't think so. It leads into a public alleyway,

you know, so I'm pretty careful about keeping it
locked."

"Do you think someone broke the window to get
in?" Muffin asked, in a voice so low she could hardly
be heard.

"I'm afraid it looks that way. Somebody broke the
windowpane, then reached in to unlock the door."

Mr. Martin looked down at the solemn, wide-eyed faces of the two girls. He put an arm about each of them and said, "What say we start looking around — to see if anything's missing?"

Nina's first thought was of Henri and Henriette. She ran into the front room to make sure they were still there. Her breath came easier when she saw the two figures behind the glass door of their cabinet.

"They look all right," said Muffin, who came up beside Nina.

"Thank goodness." Nina started to open the cabinet, then stopped and turned to Muffin. "The door wasn't closed all the way," she said. *She* always closed it till she heard it click. "Golly, Muff, do you s'pose the person that broke in . . . ?" She couldn't finish the sentence. She dreaded the idea that someone might have been tampering with her beloved dolls.

"Let's turn them on and see," suggested Muffin.

Mr. Martin came up just then. "Anything wrong there?" he asked.

"I don't think so," said Nina, flashing a look at Muffin that meant "Keep quiet."

"Well then, look around some more, will you girls? I don't notice anything missing so far." Mr.

Martin continued his search, and Nina and Muffin moved about the shop too.

At last Mr. Martin heaved a sigh of relief. "Nothing's gone that I can see," he said. "How about you?"

Both girls shook their heads.

"Good. Something scared him off, I guess. I'm lucky." Mr. Martin cast one look around and added, "Maybe there's no point calling the police if nothing's been taken. . . . Still, maybe I'll just have another look in the back to make sure. I'll cast an eye around the alleyway, too." He disappeared into the back room, leaving the girls alone.

They made a beeline for Henri and Henriette.

"Here goes," said Nina, picking up the automaton's wind-up crank. She wound up Henriette quickly, set her at first position, and pressed the starting lever.

Henriette went into action the same as always. She moved forward, lowered her pencil to the paper, and began to draw. The Swiss chalet soon appeared.

"Well, *she's* all right," said Nina, after seeing all five of Henriette's drawings. "Now for Henri." She handed Muffin the wind-up crank. "Will you do the honors?" she asked, borrowing a favorite expression of her father's.

110

Muffin wound up the boy figure. Then she reached under his coat to set the dial. "Hey," she said, "this knob seems looser than it used to."

Nina reached in and turned the knob. "It sure does." She began nibbling a fingernail out of nervousness. "Well, start him off and let's see what happens."

They both hovered over Henri anxiously after Muffin pressed the starting lever.

"He's dipping his pen in the inkwell," Muffin said.

"And shaking out the extra drops," Nina added. "So far, so good."

Henri then put his quill pen to paper, and a few seconds later he had written "Henri Bourdon."

The girls hugged him happily.

"What are you two up to?" Mr. Martin stood looking at them from the doorway to the back room.

"Nothing, Daddy," Nina said. "We just wanted to make sure Henri and Henriette were all right."

"Well, are they?"

"I think so. We're not done yet."

"All right, but shake a leg," said Mr. Martin. "I could use your help." He went forward in the shop and climbed up to finish removing the American flag from the wall.

Nina and Muffin hurried on in their examination of Henri. He went right through his five performances, and each piece of writing looked perfectly normal. After the last one, Muffin reached over to turn his dial back to its "off" position. Suddenly she made a sputtering, choking sound.

"Gleeps, Nina, you know what?" I turned the knob *forward* by mistake, and it kept right on going! It never did that before, did it?"

"Gosh, no. It never went beyond five. Let me see." Nina looked under Henri's coat at the dial. It was now pointing at a spot some distance past the final setting. "Someone *has* been fooling with him!"

"And found a sixth position?" asked Muffin in a shaky whisper. "Can Henri write something else, do you think? Something we've never seen before?"

"The message we've been looking for?" Nina breathed. She stared at Muffin in silence. Then she smiled slowly. "There's only one way to find out, isn't there?" She pressed the starting lever.

7. George Ballantine's Story

HENRI STARTED TO MOVE. He dipped his quill pen in the inkwell as before, and again snapped his hand a couple of times to shake off the extra ink. Then he brought his pen to the paper.

Nina and Muffin bent over him, hardly daring to breathe. He started to write — but no marks appeared on the paper. He moved his pen along, then stopped and raised his hand to its position of rest. The paper was still absolutely blank.

"Invisible ink?" asked Muffin, trying to figure it out.

Nina squinted into the inkwell. "Humph, just no ink at all," she said. She took a small bottle from the cabinet and poured some of the black fluid into Henri's empty inkwell. Then she set Henri going again.

This time his writing was visible. A nice black letter **c** appeared first, and Nina and Muffin grinned at each other in anticipation. After the **c** came an **a**, next a **g**, and then an **e**.

"Cage!" whispered Muffin. "What d'you know?"

"It's a good beginning, all right," agreed Nina. She smiled encouragement at Henri. "Well, go on."

Henri stared down at what he had written. But he did not go on. Slowly and a bit jerkily, he began raising his hand to show he had finished.

"Is that *all?*" cried Nina. "Aren't you going to write anything more?" She looked from Henri to Muffin in an "I-can't-believe-it" kind of way.

Muffin shook her blond head sadly. "I guess that's it. 'Cage' — what a silly thing to write! He's just telling us the same thing we know already."

"How *could* you?" Nina reproached Henri. She was suddenly very tired of never getting anywhere with this mystery. She kicked the leg of the cabinet with her slipper and then flounced off across the room.

Her father looked up from spreading his historic flag in the window. "The two H's all right?" he asked.

"Just fine," said Nina shortly.

"Good. Well, suppose you give me a hand then."

Nina and Muffin helped him with the flag until it was draped just the way he wanted it. Then he brought out another item for display: a wood-

115

framed portrait of an Early American grandmother.

Muffin studied the painting. The old woman was dressed in black. Her hair was drawn back severely, her mouth was a tight little line, and her eyes had a "no-nonsense" look about them. "I wouldn't want her for *my* grandmother," Muffin said.

Mr. Martin smiled. "Maybe she was kinder than she looks. How about bringing me those muskets?"

Nina and Muffin each shouldered a musket and marched up to the window with it. Mr. Martin arranged the guns with their barrels crossing each other. Then he stood back and inspected them. "I wonder . . ." he said. "You know that cannonball I use for a paperweight?"

"I'll get it for you, Daddy," Nina said. She went over to his desk where the old cannonball, mounted on a wooden base, was holding down a pile of papers. When she picked up the cannonball, one of the sheets of paper floated away and down to the floor. Nina stooped to retrieve it. She caught sight of something else, lying under the desk, so she picked it up too.

"Oh, just an old matchbook," she muttered. She was about to toss it into the wastebasket when she noticed the monogram on the front. In curly gold script there were the letters GB and below them the Roman numeral III.

"George Ballantine the third!" Nina gasped.

She slid the matchbook into her pocket, brought her father his cannonball, and then nudged Muffin with her elbow. "Follow me," she whispered and headed for the back room. Muffin hurried after her.

Nina brought out the matchbook to show her. Muffin gazed at the monogram engraved in gold. Then she caught her breath. "George Ballantine the third!" she exclaimed, just as Nina had done a minute earlier. "Where'd you find it?"

"Under Daddy's desk." Nina jumped into the old-fashioned sleigh and motioned Muffin in beside her. "I bet I know what happened," she said. "Daddy wouldn't sell Henri and Henriette, and Mr. Ballantine wanted them. So he broke in here at night and played them to try and get their message. He must've dropped his matchbook while he was here."

"That sounds fine," Muffin said. "Only *which* Ballantine, Brown or Red?"

Nina was stumped. "They both had matchbooks,"

117

she said, " 'cause I remember they both tried to light Daddy's cigarette." She ran her hand back and forth along the smooth wooden arm of the sleigh. Then she said, "Muff, I think we better tell Daddy about all this. I mean, now with the matchbook and the shop being broken into and everything . . ." She climbed down out of the sleigh.

"I guess you're right," said Muffin. She got up too, and together they went back into the front room.

Mr. Martin was now lifting the bust of Abraham Lincoln off its shelf.

"Daddy, please sit down," Nina said, trying to prepare him. "We have something very important to tell you."

"Don't you think I can take it standing up?" he asked with a grin. But when he saw their solemn faces, he stopped teasing. He put the bust of Lincoln back on the shelf, drew a cigarette from his platinum case, and put it in his mouth. Then he went over to his newly acquired rocking chair and sat down. Resting his hands on its curved arms, he rocked slowly back and forth. "Fire away," he said.

First Muffin told him about how the spinet-playing doll spelled out "cage" with the last four notes of her music. Then Nina explained how she had connected the word "cage" with the monkey that Henriette drew, and how she had put them together to get "monkey cage."

"Monkey cage, eh?" said Mr. Martin. He had stopped rocking. His eyes were gleaming, and he seemed to have forgotten completely that he'd told the girls to think no more about the Ballantines and their mysterious behavior.

"Well," Nina went on, "we were sure 'monkey cage' was a secret message and that's why they wanted Henri and Henriette."

"Sounds possible," Mr. Martin agreed.

"So of course we went straight to the zoo," said Muffin, "to see the monkey cages."

"And . . . ?" Mr. Martin was leaning forward eagerly, waiting to hear what happened.

"Nothing," said Nina with a scowl. "We didn't find out anything at all."

"But then we learned about a tearoom called The Monkey Cage," Muffin said. She told Mr. Martin about their visit there.

"And . . . ?" he asked again, still tilted forward in the rocker.

"Another big fat nothing," said Muffin in disgust.

"We were stuck for a while," Nina told her father. "But then we thought maybe 'monkey cage' wasn't the whole message. After all, the Ballantines didn't just want Henriette. They wanted Henri along with her. So we thought maybe *he* gave a piece of the message, too."

"Very smart," said Mr. Martin. "And what did you find out?"

"Nothing at first," Nina replied. "But when we played him just now we found something. Come see."

Mr. Martin got up, and they all trooped across the room to the automatons' cabinet.

"I found the door like this, Daddy," Nina said. She moved the cabinet door until it was just slightly ajar. "I always shut it till I hear the click. But look what Muff found." They showed him the sixth position on Henri's dial that they'd never known about before.

Mr. Martin was bobbing his head, and his cigarette was bobbing up and down with it. "Do you mean our Henri writes something we've never seen before?" he asked in amazement.

"Watch." Nina set Henri in motion again, and Mr. Martin watched him write the word "cage."

"Well, I'll be a monkey's uncle!" he exclaimed.

"I wish you were Henriette's monkey's uncle," Nina said. "Then maybe you could understand this crazy message. 'Monkey cage' and then just 'cage' again. It doesn't make any sense."

Mr. Martin frowned. "We're still in the dark then."

"Well, there's one more thing. Look what I just found under your desk." Nina took the matchbook out of her pocket and handed it to him.

Her father looked at the monogram. "Hmm. George Ballantine the third, do you think?"

"We sure do," said Muffin.

"Don't you see, Daddy?" Nina rushed on. "You wouldn't sell Henri and Henriette to Mr. Ballantine. So he finally broke in here to see if he could find their secret message. And . . ."

"Now hold on a minute," cut in Mr. Martin. "That's a fine-sounding theory, but actually either one of the Ballantines could've dropped this matchbook when he was here last week. My cleaning woman doesn't always get underneath the desk."

"I s'pose," Nina admitted grudgingly. "But *I* bet he dropped it last night." She chewed away at a fingernail for a moment and then said, "Look. Somebody broke in. Nothing's missing, so it wasn't a burglar. Whoever it was, he was playing with Henri. And the only people who've looked at Henri and Henriette in years are the Ballantines!" Nina finished with a triumphant wave of her hand.

"Your logic is good, puss," her father said. "So let's assume you're right. Our next question is . . ."

"*Which* Ballantine?" Nina and Muffin chorused along with him.

They all looked at one another helplessly.

They were still looking at one another helplessly when they heard a fierce screeching of car brakes. Nina ran to the window and saw that a taxicab had stopped right in front of their door. Then she saw a man get out of the cab. She wheeled around frantically. "Brown Ballantine!" she cried.

Sure enough, in strode that very man. "I hope I'm not interrupting anything, Mr. Martin," he said. "I'm just on the way home from Penn Station. My cab passed right by here and so I thought . . ."

"That's quite all right," Mr. Martin interrupted,

walking toward him. "We're just arranging a new window display." He made a show of searching through all his pockets and then added, "I seem to be out of matches. Could I trouble you for a light?"

Nina and Muffin stared at each other. Mr. Martin hadn't lit a cigarette in years. He'd even told Mr. Ballantine that last week. What could he be thinking of?

"Thought you didn't smoke," said Mr. Ballantine, reaching for his matches anyway.

"I don't really, but it's been a tough week." Nina's father took the matchbook and, as he held it up to light his cigarette, Nina and Muffin understood. They, too, saw the initials GB and the Roman numeral III.

"I won't keep you — I've got a cab waiting," said Mr. Ballantine. "I just wondered if by any chance you'd changed your mind about selling the automatons. I meant to stop in sooner, but I've been out of town the last few days."

Out of town the last few days . . . Was he telling the truth? If so, Nina thought to herself, it must have been Red Ballantine who broke in last night.

Mr. Martin seemed to be thinking along the same

lines as his daughter. "Mr. Ballantine," he said, facing him squarely, "can you prove who you are and where you were last night?"

Mr. Ballantine's eyes positively bulged. "Well, I must say," he spluttered, "that *is* an odd thing to ask. However," he went on, smiling, "if answering it will help me get the automatons, I'll oblige."

He reached into an inside pocket of his jacket and drew out a dark leather wallet. From the wallet he began to produce identification. He handed Mr. Martin a driver's license, a registration card from the New York Athletic Club, and a military identification card complete with photograph.

There could be no doubt now that this man was George Ballantine III.

"As for last night," he said, "I think I've still got my hotel bill on me somewhere." He fished through other pockets, bringing out, among other things, a silver cigarette case and a handkerchief with the same monogram as on the matchbook. Finally he unfolded a bill stamped "paid" for last night and several nights before at the Barclay Hotel in Philadelphia.

"Thank you," said Mr. Martin, giving a token puff on his cigarette. "I'll tell you now why I played police inspector with you. Someone broke in here last night and fooled around with my automatons, and I was afraid it might've been you."

"Me? Why me? Surely I'm not the only person who's shown an interest in your automatons," Mr. Ballantine said in disbelief.

Mr. Martin shook his head slowly. "No, there's one other person . . . Tell me this, Mr. Ballantine: could anyone possibly have been using your apartment while you were away?"

"Yes, as a matter of fact, there *was* someone there. But how did you know that?" He looked Mr. Martin up and down as though searching for his crystal ball. "My friend Henry Wilbur has been staying with me for a couple of months. Why?"

"Does he have red hair?" Nina blurted out.

Mr. Ballantine stared at her in surprise. "Yes, he does. What is this?"

"There's a simple explanation." Mr. Martin, with Nina and Muffin helping, told him about Mr. Wilbur's visits to the shop and their visit to Mr. Wilbur's.

"He called himself George Ballantine the third," Nina said.

"And he wanted to buy the automatons," added Muffin.

To everyone's amazement, Mr. Ballantine didn't seem at all upset. In fact, he laughed. "Good old Red," he said. "He must have been planning to surprise me." He looked at the three bewildered faces in front of him and added, "Maybe I'd better tell you the story."

Before he could begin, though, the door of the shop opened and a man stuck his head in. "Hey Mac," he called, "you still want to hold my cab?"

Mr. Ballantine winked at Nina and Muffin. "Forgot all about him." In a louder voice, he called back to the cabby, "Yes, if you don't mind. I won't be long."

"Okay by me," said the cab driver, and he disappeared.

"Please tell us the story, Mr. Ballantine," Nina urged, afraid he might not want to run up the taxi meter any higher.

"Oh yes, please do," echoed Muffin. She gave him her most dazzling smile.

"It's a rather long story, I'm afraid," said Mr. Ballantine, "but I'll make it as short as I can." He perched on the edge of an Early American settle. Nina and Muffin darted over to sit down on either side of him, and Mr. Martin pulled up his rocker.

"When my grandfather died many years ago," began Mr. Ballantine, "he left, along with his will, a strange note. The note was in triplicate — one copy for each of his three sons. This is what it said:

> A fortune have I left for whichever of you is clever enough to find it. I have entrusted the secret of its whereabouts to some friends of mine who will never speak a word of it."

Mr. Ballantine looked at the wide-eyed faces of Nina and Muffin, and he smiled. "My father and his two brothers must've looked just as surprised as you when they first read the note."

"But did they find the fortune?" Nina asked.

"No, they never did. Though I doubt if they tried very hard. You see," Mr. Ballantine continued, "in the first place, he had already left them quite a bit of money. And secondly, my granddad was a great practical joker. So after his sons had poked around a bit without success, they figured the note was probably just another one of his jokes."

"It wasn't though, I bet," said Muffin solemnly.

"Perhaps not," agreed Mr. Ballantine. "But in any case, the matter was finally dropped. In fact, it lay dead and buried right up until about two months ago."

"What happened then?" piped Nina and Muffin almost in unison.

"Well, one night a couple of months ago I was listening to my automaton playing her minuet. I'm not very musical," Mr. Ballantine said, "but still I like to hear her play. Anyway, that night it suddenly struck me that the four notes at the very end didn't really seem to belong."

Nina and Muffin looked at each other triumphantly. Mr. Martin tipped an imaginary hat to them both.

"I got to wondering what those notes were doing there," Mr. Ballantine went on. "Finally it occurred to me to find out what the notes were. So I asked my friend Red Wilbur — he'd just come to stay with me for a while, and he knows a little about music. Red listened, and you can imagine my surprise when he told me the notes spelled out the word 'cage'!"

"Muffin figured out 'cage' right away when she heard the minuet," Nina couldn't resist telling him.

"You did?" said Mr. Ballantine. "I congratulate you. It took years before I suspected anything."

"Well, I play the piano," said Muffin modestly. "What happened after you got 'cage'?"

"Nothing for a while," answered Mr. Ballantine. "Then, when I was going through my desk one day, I came upon my grandfather's old note to his sons. And as I looked at it, an idea came to me. Suppose those 'friends' in the note were Granddad's three automatons? He loved them enough to call them friends. And while they would never speak, as the note said, they could still tell a secret through their actions. Why, Granddad could easily have had those extra four notes added. Collecting mechanical objects was a great hobby with him, and he knew a lot of expert craftsmen in the field."

Nina and Muffin were following Mr. Ballantine's words so intently that they sat like rigid little poles on either side of him.

"Then I said to myself," he went on, "if the musical doll spells out a word on her keyboard, then maybe the other two dolls tell part of the secret through their drawings and writings. Perhaps, I thought, my granddad hadn't been joking after all. Perhaps he *had* left a hidden fortune!"

"But you didn't have the other two dolls," Nina said. "So how could you find out?"

"The problem in a nutshell," replied Mr. Ballantine, waggling his long index finger at her. "The other two had been sold by my father long ago. I had to find them."

He searched among his father's papers, he told them, and found out who had bought the dolls. He went to see that person, only to learn that the dolls had long since been sold again — to an antique dealer named Martin.

"So now you know why I came to your shop," Mr. Ballantine finished. "And why I wanted the automatons so badly. I was going to tell you all this, anyway, if you kept on refusing me."

"But Red Wilbur . . ." Nina began.

"Red Wilbur knows the whole story," Mr. Ballantine said. "He wanted to surprise me, I guess — have the automations waiting for me when I got back from my trip."

Nina and Muffin made faces at each other. They had very different ideas about what Red Wilbur wanted to do.

"Why would he break in here?" Nina asked. "He wouldn't do something against the law just to surprise you, would he?"

Mr. Ballantine, in turn, didn't believe that Red Wilbur had broken into the shop. Even when Nina showed him the matchbook with the monogram GB III, he just shrugged. "Oh, those matchbooks of mine, they're all over the apartment. Red and I both use them — either of us could've dropped this one here last week."

"Still" — Mr. Martin came in on the side of Nina and Muffin — "somebody broke in and fiddled with the automatons. And you and Mr. Wilbur are the only people who've been interested in them in years."

"Hmm. I can't believe that Red . . ." Mr. Ballantine got up and went over to look at the automatons. The Martins and Muffin followed him.

Nina introduced the dolls to Mr. Ballantine. "This is Henri. He's the one that writes," she said proudly. "And this is Henriette — she's the artist and she's terrific." Nina gave them each an affectionate squeeze. "If we show you everything they do, you won't still want to buy them, will you?"

Mr. Ballantine looked down at the young girl's anxious face. "Perhaps not, after all," he said gently.

"Well, then," said Muffin through a grin, "what are we waiting for? Secret message, here we come."

"Remember me, buddy?" called a voice just then.

"You still want me to wait? Meter's at two forty now."

Nina and Muffin glared at the cab driver, who was standing in the doorway. Was he going to spoil everything for them? Why couldn't he have waited a few minutes longer?

Happily, though, Mr. Ballantine said, "Fine, fine. Won't be much longer." Then he turned back eagerly to the mechanical figures.

"It's *your* money," said the driver, and out he went again.

"Here goes Henri, Mr. Ballantine," Nina said. "Look." She pressed the starting lever, and the boy figure went into his act.

"Excellent!" cried Mr. Ballantine, as he saw the name Henri Bourdon appear on the paper.

"Oh, that's nothing," said Nina. "Watch this." She put Henri through his paces, and Mr. Ballantine grew more and more enthusiastic. At the end, though, his face clouded over. "He's a talented little boy, but I don't see any clue to Granddad's fortune, do you?"

"Well, there's one thing you haven't seen yet," Nina told him. "We hadn't either, till today. Red

Wilbur found" — Nina caught herself — "whoever it was that broke in — found a sixth position for Henri. Look." She showed him that latest discovery — Henri writing the word "cage."

"Why, how very odd," said Mr. Ballantine. "The same word my automaton spells out with her notes." He rubbed his chin thoughtfully. "I can't see any reason for repeating it."

"We couldn't either," said Muffin.

"Well, what about the girl here?" Mr. Ballantine patted the top of Henriette's blond head. "Maybe she'll shed some light on the matter."

"She does draw one thing that's always puzzled us," Mr. Martin told him. "Maybe it'll make some sense to you."

Henriette took the stage. She lowered her pencil to the paper and began to sketch out her delicate Swiss chalet.

"It's lovely," said Mr. Ballantine, "but I can't see anything strange about it."

Henriette drew her Swiss town hall with its spire and big clock.

"Nothing strange about that either," murmured Mr. Ballantine.

133

"How about this, though?" asked Nina, as Henriette began to draw her speak-no-evil monkey.

George Ballantine the third stared down at the picture. The color drained from his face, and in a queer, shaky voice he said, "Monkey . . . cage." Then he looked up, wild-eyed, at Nina and Muffin and Mr. Martin.

"Follow me, all of you!" he cried. "We haven't a second to lose!"

8. The Mystery Is Solved

Mr. Ballantine bolted for the door. He bumped into the potted palm, banging his shin. Then he tripped over a brass bedstead, stubbing his toe. He groaned, but kept going. At the door, he ran smack into the cab driver, who was just popping his head into the shop for the third time. They both landed in a heap on the floor.

Nina and Muffin rushed up, crying, "Are you hurt?" Mr. Martin helped them to their feet.

Mr. Ballantine wiggled his arms and legs, checking for injuries. Then he walked a few steps. Everything still seemed to be in working order. "I'm sorry," he said to the cab driver. I —"

"S'all right," said the cabby, who had also been making sure he was in one piece. "No bones broken. Only, tell me, buddy — where's the fire all of a sudden? You make me wait an hour, and then wham! you come streaking out like a rocket."

This reminded Mr. Ballantine that he was in a hurry. He picked up his hat and clapped it back on his head. "Let's go, folks!" he cried, and dashed out to the waiting cab. The others streamed after him.

The taxi was one of the big, old-fashioned kind, with room enough in the back for jump seats. Nina and Muffin each pulled down one and plunked onto it so they could face the two men in the back seat.

The cab no sooner began to move than Nina pounced. "Mr. Ballantine," she said, "what do you know that we don't know? We couldn't get anywhere with 'monkey cage.' "

"No, of course you couldn't." Mr. Ballantine was sitting straight as a rod in his seat. He looked as though he would like nothing better than to dive forward and grab the wheel of the cab. "Can't you go faster, driver?" he asked.

"Not and keep my license, chief," said the driver, unruffled. "I'm doin' the limit now."

Mr. Ballantine heaved a loud sigh and shifted

nervously in his seat. Nina and Muffin were both gazing at him expectantly.

"Monkey cage," said Nina as a reminder.

"Sure enough. Do you remember all those cages I showed you in the 'museum'?"

"Of course," Nina said, her eyes glowing. "With the wonderful mechanical birds inside. We thought of them, but they're *bird* cages, not *monkey* cages."

"All but *one* are bird cages," Mr. Ballantine corrected her. "One of those cages originally housed a mechanical monkey. A great fellow he was, too. Did all sorts of tricks. Acrobatics on the crossbar, swinging by his tail . . ."

"Gleeps," broke in Muffin. Then she almost fell off her jump seat as the taxi lurched to a stop at a red light. She righted herself and went on, "You think the fortune's in that cage then, Mr. Ballantine?"

"I wouldn't be at all surprised," he said. "Is that light going to stay red all day?" He fidgeted in his seat and moaned a little. "What worries me," he said, "is that Red Wilbur knows about the cage that held the mechanical monkey. So if it *was* Red who broke in and fiddled with Henri and Henriette —"

"Then he might've figured out the message 'monkey cage,'" Nina broke in. "Why, he might be finding the fortune in the cage at this very moment."

The red light changed to green and the cab shot forward.

"At this very moment," repeated Mr. Ballantine in a somber tone. "Although I can still hardly believe that Red . . ." He trailed off, scowling and shaking his head.

"But . . ." began Nina, and then stopped as she caught her father's eye. He was looking at her in a way that said, "Better not bother him right now."

Nina obeyed, but it was hard. There were so many things she wanted to know. Fortunately, though, she didn't have very long to wait. The cab jolted to a stop in front of the Ballantine house.

"Well, at last," said Mr. Ballantine. He was all ready with his money. He thrust the bills at the driver, grabbed his suitcase, and leaped out of the cab. He was taking the steps of his brownstone house two by two while the others were still getting out of the taxi.

Nina, Muffin, and Mr. Martin followed in Mr. Ballantine's wake. Up the steps they charged, through the two doors, and up the carpeted staircase till they reached the top floor. Mr. Ballantine was turning the key just as they got there. The door opened, and they all burst into the apartment.

They stood together in the dim foyer for a second. Then Mr. Ballantine raised a forefinger and said, "Listen!" From the living room ahead of them came a clink-clink like the sound of a hammer striking metal. They all made for the living room as one.

It was a strange sight that greeted them. There, on the middle of the rug, sat Red Wilbur. He looked very sad. In one hand he held a screwdriver, and a hammer lay beside him. Beside him was a large white cage, and the red carpet all around it was strewn with flakes of white paint.

"Red!" gasped Mr. Ballantine. He couldn't say any more — he just stared in grief at the scene before him.

Red Wilbur was clearly amazed to see George Ballantine. He dropped both hammer and screwdriver and staggered to his feet. "G-George!" he moaned. "How . . .? W-what? You weren't due back till tomorrow!"

"By which time you planned to be far away," said Mr. Ballantine. "*With* my grandfather's fortune." His voice showed the bitterness he felt at his friend's betrayal.

To Nina and Muffin's surprise, Red Wilbur didn't try to deny it. He just said a very low and quivery "Yes." He ran his hands through his red hair, which already looked as though hands had been combing through it for quite a while. He seemed about to burst into tears.

"George," he said, his voice still wobbling, "I've

done something terrible. I've betrayed your friend-
ship. I impersonated you in order to get the automatons. I went to the antique shop, posing as you,
when you were supposed to be going out of town.
Then when you postponed your trip, I waited till
you finally did go and then I went back to the shop.
I even invited these people here. Wore a wig to
change the color of my hair. But they wouldn't sell

me the automatons," he babbled on, "so I finally broke into the antique shop last night. Oh, I wasn't going to steal" — he saw the look of horror on George's face — "I just wanted to find the secret message."

Mr. Ballantine looked from his false friend to the cage on the floor. "I see you were successful."

"Well, I *thought* so, George,"said the distraught Wilbur. "But now I wonder. I've been working on this confounded cage for hours. All in vain." His hands fluttered in a gesture of helplessness. "No secret panel, no false bottom, no hidden compartment. If your grandfather hid something in here, George, I give up. I can't find it." He tapped the cage with the toe of his shoe and added, "..This *was* the cage with the monkey, wasn't it?"

"It's the one, all right," said Mr. Ballantine. He turned to Nina's father. "You see, Mr. Martin, it's heavier than a bird cage, and the bars are much thicker. Granddad was very careful about details. This cage was for a monkey, so it had to look stronger than the bird cages."

Mr. Martin, Nina, and Muffin were all examining the cage, and Red Wilbur stood back a little, shifting from one foot to the other uncomfortably.

"Say, George," Wilbur said suddenly, "where *is*

that mechanical monkey? Maybe that's where your fortune is hidden — inside the monkey!"

This sounded like a terrific idea to Nina and Muffin, but Mr. Ballantine threw up his hands hopelessly. "If that's the answer," he said, "we can forget about the fortune once and for all. I used to play with the monkey when I was a boy. I broke it finally, and it was thrown away."

Nina and Muffin let out long "ohs" of disappointment. Mr. Ballantine gave them a wan smile. "I'm as disappointed as you are," he told them. "But it looks as if we'll have to label this case 'unsolved.'"

Disappointed though he was about that, he seemed even sadder at Red Wilbur's treachery. "Red," he said dismally, "how could you?"

Red Wilbur seemed genuinely sorry. Beads of perspiration dampened his forehead, and he dabbed at them with his handkerchief. "I never would've done it, I swear it, George," he said, "but I'm in a very bad jam." In gloomy tones he started to tell a black tale about his finances.

Mr. Martin cleared his throat. "Well, girls," he said, "we'd better be on our way. It doesn't look as though we can be of any more use here." He turned to say good-bye to Mr. Ballantine.

Nina fought back tears. To be *this* close to solving the mystery and then have it all come to nothing! Wasn't there something they were overlooking — something that would put them on the track of the hidden fortune? She had the feeling that all the pieces of the puzzle were there. If only she could fit them together!

Slowly Nina followed her father and Muffin out of Mr. Ballantine's living room. She was almost at the door when the idea came to her.

"Listen, everybody!" she cried. "I've just thought of something!"

Muffin wheeled around. Mr. Martin turned back too. George Ballantine and Red Wilbur were standing, staring at her, near the monkey cage.

"Well?" asked Muffin.

"What is it?" asked Mr. Ballantine.

"Out with it, Nina," said her father.

Nina smiled mysteriously. "There's one thing we've never figured out in all of this," she said.

"Which is?" encouraged Mr. Ballantine.

Nina turned to him. "Which is — why your grandfather would have used the word 'cage' twice. Your doll spells out 'cage' on her spinet, and Henri writes 'cage.' Why both of them?"

Four pairs of shoulders shrugged despairingly.

"You said just now that your grandfather was very careful about details," Nina went on. "So he must have had a reason for the two 'cages.'"

"Sounds logical," agreed Mr. Ballantine. "Only what's the reason?"

"Well," Nina said, "Maybe he meant to say 'monkey-cage cage.'" Everyone looked blank.

"Don't you see?" Nina explained. "If you repeated the word 'cage,' maybe he was doing it to draw attention to the cage itself. Maybe he was saying it was the *cage itself* that was the fortune."

"That old steel cage?" Mr. Ballantine gave a snort of disbelief. "Not very likely, I'm afraid."

Still, they all started re-examining the cage. Certainly it didn't *look* valuable. It seemed to be just an ordinary steel cage, painted white, with the metal showing here and there where Red Wilbur's hammering had flaked off the paint.

"No, I don't see —" began Mr. Ballantine.

"*I* do!" exclaimed Mr. Martin. He was bending over the cage, peering closely at the exposed metal of the bars. He stepped back, pulled his cigarette case from his pocket, and held it out.

"No thanks," said Mr. Ballantine.

Mr. Martin grinned. "I wasn't offering you a cigarette. I was showing you the case."

"What about it, Daddy?" Nina asked. "It's your same old platinum case, isn't it?"

"None other." He gripped one of the bars of the monkey cage. "And these bars. . . ."

"Oh, they're platinum too!" cried Nina.

"Yes, by Jove," said her father. "Unless I miss my guess, Mr. Ballantine, that cage of yours is worth a whopping sum."

Mr. Ballantine ran his hands lovingly along the platinum bars. "So here is Granddad's fortune," he murmured. "At long last." Then he began to laugh.

"What's so funny, Mr. Ballantine?" Nina asked.

He grinned at her. "A fortune in the bars of a monkey cage — it's just Granddad's kind of joke. He would have loved all the trouble we had finding it, too. And do you know," he said to Nina, "I think he would've gotten a real kick out of the fact that, in spite of all the grownups around, it was *you* who finally solved the mystery."

Mr. Ballantine stared at Nina, and he grew solemn for a moment. "Miss Martin, I don't know how to thank you." Then suddenly he smiled. "Yes," he said. "Yes, perhaps I do know how."

9. A Beautiful Surprise

"Go solve a mystery, and what does it get you," Nina grumbled. "You're still treated like a slave." She managed to look properly wounded as she faced her mother.

Mrs. Martin just smiled and gave her a small push. "Go on, dear. Those dresser drawers of yours are crying to be put in order. You haven't straightened them in months."

"I don't hear them crying," Nina said. But she shuffled out of the living room, resigning herself to the dreaded chore.

In her bedroom, she stood before the chest of

drawers that her father had given her two years ago. It was made of dark walnut, and ordinarily she was very fond of it. At the moment though, she wouldn't have been sorry to see the floor open up and swallow it.

Nina yanked open one drawer after the other. She winced. Her mother had a point — a family of rats would be right at home in any one of them. The bottom drawer was a shade neater than the others, so Nina chose it first. She pulled it out, set it down on her bed, and dug in.

Not long afterward the door chimes pealed out "Oh, say, can you see." Nina dropped a pile of blouses and ran to see who was there. She found her mother opening the door for Muffin.

"Extra! Extra! Read all about it!" piped Muffin. She held a newspaper out in front of her, and Nina gasped when she saw it. The headline said, in huge black letters:

NINA MARTIN SOLVES
MYSTERY OF HIDDEN FORTUNE!

"Oh, Muff!" Nina cried, and she grabbed the paper to read the story. But there was no story.

Under the exciting headline there were various items of news, but not another mention of Nina Martin and her solving the mystery.

"I don't understand." Nina looked from the paper to Muffin. Then she saw a familiar gleam in her friend's blue eyes.

"Now I've finally fooled *you* too," Muffin said triumphantly. "Yippee!"

Nina thrust the newspaper back at Muffin angrily. "You had that headline printed up, didn't you?" She was beginning to understand the trick. "In one of those novelty stores on Broadway?"

Muffin, grinning, nodded.

"You're a rat," Nina told her flatly.

"I think it was a lovely idea," said Mrs. Martin. "You can frame it, dear, and hang it in your room."

"Um, that's true." Nina cooled off a little. "Well, come on in, Muff," she said rather grudgingly, "and let's see where it'll look best."

Mrs. Martin went into the kitchen to get dinner under way. "Don't forget those drawers," she called over her shoulder.

Muffin held the newspaper up over Nina's bed. Nina studied it and then said "No." They tried the wall above Nina's bookcase. Nina decided against that too. She finally chose a spot over her walnut dresser. "This way I'll be able to see it first thing when I wake up," she said.

Then Muffin helped with the straightening of the dresser drawers. She was very quick and neat. Nina's last remaining bit of anger vanished after that. "Thanks, Muff," she said. "It would've taken me *hours*."

"Any time . . . I better blow now." Muffin started for the door. "We're having dinner soon."

The girls left Nina's bedroom together. They got to the living room just in time to see Mr. Martin staggering through the front door with a large box.

Four young eyes stared eagerly at the box. It was about three feet square and wrapped in brown paper. Mr. Martin set it down on the living-room floor and then turned away.

"Aren't you going to open it, Daddy?" Nina asked.

He shook his head. "Can't. It's not addressed to me." He began to grin, and Nina bent down to read the label.

"It's for me!" she cried.

"It arrived at the shop this afternoon," her father told her.

150

Nina stood stockstill, gazing at the big package. "Who'd be sending *me* something?" she asked. "And what could it be?"

Muffin wriggled with impatience. "We'll never know if you don't open it."

"True. I'll get the scissors." When she came back with them, her mother and father and Muffin were all hovering like hawks over the surprise package.

Cord was cut. Paper was torn. At last Nina was able to fold back the top of the box and look down into it. She saw nothing but a huge mass of excelsior and crumpled newspaper. Excited, she started to plunge her arms in.

"Hold on a minute," her father said, "maybe I can get it out for you." He took off his jacket and reached his shirtsleeved arms gingerly down among the packing. He felt around for a moment with his eyes shut in concentration, and then he suddenly opened his eyes and grinned broadly at Nina. "Get ready, puss," he said. "Here it comes." He gave a great heave and lifted a large object straight up out of the box. Excelsior and newspaper fell in all directions.

"Chester — my rug!" wailed Mrs. Martin. But she bent over the large object just as eagerly as all the

151

rest of them as Mr. Martin set it on the marble coffee table.

It was about two feet high and thickly wrapped in white paper. Nina began peeling off the tissue very carefully.

"Gleeps!" shouted Muffin.

Nina gave a small, short squeak.

There on the coffee table was the Ballantine doll, sitting at her spinet, fingers on the keys, ready to play her minuet.

"Look, Nina," said her mother. She pointed to a tiny envelope tied around one of the legs of the spinet.

Nina untied the envelope, opened it, and drew out a white card.

"For Nina Martin," it read, "with my deepest gratitude." It was signed "George Ballantine III."

Mrs. Martin read the card and handed it to her husband. "What a nice thing for him to do, Chester," she said.

Nina didn't hear. She was two hundred years away. She had pressed the starting lever, and the lovely old minuet had begun.